THE WEREWOLVES OF BROOKLYN : SIEGE OF THE DOKKALFAR

LEKHAA MEENAKSHISUNDARAM

This book is dedicated to every young supernatural lover.

Welcome and prepare to fall in love.

Contents

Acknowledgements	*vii*
Author's Note	*ix*
1. Chapter 1	1
2. Chapter 2	10
3. Chapter 3	15
4. Chapter 4	19
5. Chapter 5	29
6. Chapter 6	34
7. Chapter 7	42
8. Chapter 8	47
9. Chapter 9	59
10. Chapter 10	65
11. Chapter 11	73
12. Chapter 12	83
13. Chapter 13	92
14. Chapter 14	98
15. Chapter 15	102
16. Chapter 16	111
17. Chapter 17	117
18. Chapter 18	124
19. Chapter 19	130
20. Chapter 20	136
21. Chapter 21	141
About the Author	147

Acknowledgements

There are so many people who helped create this book and even more who made sure I could write it.

My first thanks would undoubtedly go to my little sister for being the very first person to read my book. She read the first page of my first draft and told me that she found it interesting. She said she was curious to know what would happen next.

Writing this book would have been impossible without the constant support I had from Anderlin, my best friend. He supported me in my endeavors from the very beginning. He was a source of inspiration and my rock when things were tough. I wouldn't have made it to this stage without the belief you placed in me. Thank you for being my everlasting source of inspiration and support.

Next, I have to thank my aunt who was the first person who told me that I should try writing. On a similar note, I wouldn't be here without my favorite English teacher from school, Usha Bai Ma'am, who was very encouraging of my writing (even though she only saw my writing on tests and exams).

I have to extend my immense gratitude to my ride-or-die girls, Bowrnaa and Praveshika. They don't know I'm publishing this now (it's a surprise), but I know how ecstatic they would be when they see my name in print. They are the girls you meet in school and become your sisters. They are a part of me and they celebrate my successes like their own.

Then, I have to thank Aniketh. His playful teasing comments urged me to write. He told me that I wouldn't get anywhere if I kept falling into the world of fantasy. Now, here I am, an author of a children's fantasy book. Thank you for giving me the urge to prove myself.

Let me take a moment to thank Veena and Kavin. These people showed as much enthusiasm as I did when they found out I was going to publish my work. I have to thank them for this. I also have to thank Sharan and Shane, my seniors who, along with my brother, were one of the reasons I settled into college. I don't think I would have had the confidence to do this if they hadn't helped me rediscover it. Thank you to Saru, who was there for me when I needed company the most. He showed me that people can genuinely care.

My magnanimous thanks to my professors, Dr. Samuel Rufus and Professor Phebe Angus. Dr. Samuel Rufus for giving me the opportunity to publish and for helping me throughout the journey. To Professor Phebe Angus for extending her supporting arm as soon as she heard I was writing. I also have to thank my mentor, Professor Monsingh Daniel for encouraging me when he heard of my endeavor.

While we are talking about teachers, I have to thank my 10th-grade teachers, Geetha Ma'am, Kavitha Ma'am, and Vimala Ma'am. They instilled something in me that's pretty intangible. They are an important part of who I am today.

How could I forget to thank my beta reader, Ann Mariya? She accepted my request as soon as I posed it and she encouraged me when she said she loved my work. She helped me believe in myself and in my work.

A huge thanks to Titus, for creating a magnificent cover design.

I can't continue without thanking my senior, Shreya Prasath. She published a book just before I did and she gave me a bunch of helpful suggestions. A huge thanks to Sethu Parvathy for her immediate enthusiasm.

I could never forget Taylor Swift here. Her music helped me through my writer's block. A massive thanks to Twilight, The Vampire Diaries, and Teen Wolf for merging together to inspire my writing. To Rick Riordan for showing me that people love mythology.

Last but not least, I'd like to extend an immense thanks to everyone holding this book. Thank you for giving my work a chance.

Author's Note

Dear reader,

When I first started writing this, I was in my 'supernatural' phase. I loved watching and reading things related to the world of the supernatural. I was also a mythology lover. This book is a mixture of the supernatural and mythological worlds, that's suitable for young readers.

There are a lot of books involving various kinds of mythology. However, when you think of the world of the supernatural, all the media and material that comes to mind is A-rated. I wanted this first book to be different. I wanted it to be something that would be appropriate for a child around 12 or 13 years old, which was around the age my little sister was when I started writing. I wanted my book to be an appropriate introduction to the world I fell in love with.

I also wanted this book to showcase the love a sister can have for her brothers. This platonic bond is something that means the world to me. I realized that there aren't many books that I've read that show the beauty of that bond. I wanted to try to show the unconditional love that brothers and sisters share, even if they aren't related by blood.

I had loads of fun writing this book and it certainly won't be my last. I hope you enjoy reading my work as much as I enjoyed writing it.

With loads of love,

Lekhaa

I lived in a spacious 4-bedroom apartment with my dad, Nicolas Morgan. There was a room for Dad, one for me, a guest room, and a spare room. My name was Andrea Morgan. I dressed in jeans, a tank top, and a shirt. I made sure my outfit covered the odd birthmark I had on the front of my shoulder. It was a well-defined pawprint with a dagger through it. I covered it whenever I could.

I brushed my hair, which also had a unique feature. My lustrous amber hair had a streak of deep black. It couldn't be dyed and grew naturally with the rest of my locks. It was a big deal to me a few years ago, so much that I even considered a wig. Now I was comfortable with it. I was glad to have something to set me apart from everyone else. I grabbed my phone and backpack and went to the kitchen to see my dad wearing an apron over his white shirt. He was an executive assistant director of the FBI.

"Hey kiddo," he greeted with his usual wide smile. He dried his hands on his apron as I approached him.

"Hey Dad, good morning," I greeted. This was normal at my house. Dad and I were pretty close.

There was a much-expected knock on my door.

"Jack," my dad and I said looking at each other.

Jackson Russell was my best friend. We'd known each other since the first grade. He knew me better than anyone in the whole world, better than even my dad. We knew each other's passions, dreams, likes and dislikes. I knew what made him tick and I knew how to calm him down. Those are just things you pick up, being friends as long as we both had been. I never kept anything from Jack and he never kept anything from me. We had no secrets from each other.

Jack's parents were divorced and he lived with his mom, Calista. She worked with the NYPD. Jack was a tall tan guy with soft brown hair and blue eyes. He was a nerdy guy who just traded his glasses for contacts. He was a great soccer player, in my opinion, but never made it on the team because of his personal enmity with the captain. Jack was picked on a lot. I hoped it would stop if he got on the team.

"Hey, Andie. Hey, Mr. M," Jack called. He was totally at ease here. This was just as much his house as it was mine.

"Hey, Jack. Do you want some breakfast?" my dad asked considerately.

"No thanks," Jack replied, "Andie are you ready?"

"Yeah. Bye, Dad."

My dad waved as we went down to Jack's jeep. I got the passenger seat and he looked me up and down.

"What?" I asked defensively.

"Where's your cheer uniform?" he demanded. I was cheer captain and head of the school dance committee. I loved being a leader. It came naturally to me and I was confident that no one could lead like I did.

"Cheer practice is after school today, 'cause of soccer try-outs during the day."

"That makes sense."

"This is your year," I said, referring to him trying out for the soccer team. We'd been having this discussion on and off for days now. I might be biased but I believed that Jack deserved to be on the team. He worked really hard and would be over the moon if he got on the team.

"Yeah, my year to get a few ribs broken, Andie," he retorted, rolling his eyes at me.

"You'll be fine, Jack. I signed you up for try-outs, and you're going. End of discussion."

"You're not taking no for an answer, are you?" he sighed, exasperated. He shot me a glare as he drove.

"Of course not," I smirked at him and knew I was winning this round.

Jack pulled into the school parking lots and I gracefully slipped out of the jeep. "I'll see you at try-outs," I said, rushing to my first class. I sat in between two of my friends, Allison and Katie. Our other friend, Sophia sat behind me. They were on the cheer team with me.

"Hey guys," I said.

"Hey, captain. Are we going to watch those hot guys on the field later?" Allison asked referring to the soccer try-outs, which was all everyone would talk about today.

"I'll be there, but not as cheer captain." I didn't want my position to influence Jack's chances in any way. I just wanted to be there to support him.

"You guys are welcome to join me though."

The bell rang and our teacher walked in. She started teaching and the door opened again. Jack rushed in, disheveled. He was carrying a pile of books and the tip of his foot caught on the doorjamb. He tripped and the whole class erupted in laughter. I hid my face in my hands. I couldn't watch him in such discomfort. His face reddened and he stood up and collected his books. I watched through my fingers as he regained his composure and took his seat.

"Thank you for joining us, Mr. Russell. What was so important that you couldn't get to class on time?" the teacher demanded.

"Sorry. I was trying to get out of soccer try-outs. I couldn't," he admitted, without looking up.

"Ooooh. Be ready to get your butt kicked," the captain, Liam catcalled.

"Shut up, Liam. I've been practicing," Jack said, his blush deepening.

"That's enough boys. Save it for the soccer field," the teacher intervened. I was really thankful that she did that.

I was on my way out to the field after 3rd period. Jack was coming out of the boys' locker room in a t-shirt and shorts. He had his cleats slung over his shoulder as he tightened the straps on his shin guards. I turned his face, forcing him to look at me.

"You were trying to get out of try-outs," I stated, demanding an explanation. I thought he knew that I would only do the best for him. I knew I shouldn't have forced him into trying out, but I was so sure it would be good for him.

"You heard Liam. He and Oliver are going to humiliate me and then Liam's going to ask you to the dance this Friday." Oliver was Liam's best friend and soccer vice-captain. I didn't have anything against Oliver other than the fact that he constantly helped Liam humiliate Jack.

"Okay, first of all, I wouldn't go with Liam. Number two, you're good enough to make it Jack. If not, I'll bribe the coach to let you play," I smirked.

"Gee, Thanks, Andie. It's nice to see you believe in me so much," he said rolling his eyes at me again.

"Jack, c'mon. You know I was kidding. You'll do great."

We saw Liam crack his knuckles as Jack and I reached the edge of the field. I started biting my nails, worried for Jack.

I climbed the bleachers and took a seat. The stands filled up quickly. If you made the team, you instantly topped the popularity charts. Every girl wanted a soccer star to be their date for the dance. Every guy wanted to know who they were up against. Regardless of who you were, you wanted to know who made the team.

The coach blew his whistle and the first thing Liam did was kick the ball at Jack's chest. He was pushed a few feet back.

"Get back in there, Russell," the coach ordered. Jack stood, shook his head to clear it, dusted off his shorts, and joined the scrimmage again. He was doing pretty well.

About a half hour later, Jack faced the stands, looking in my direction but not at me. I looked around and found Katie a few feet away from me. Jack had a huge crush on her. Liam took advantage of Jack's distraction and punted the ball in Jack's direction.

"Look out!" I exclaimed. He obviously couldn't hear me. The ball hit Jack's head and he fell flat on his back, on the hard ground.

"Nerds should stay out of the field," one of the guys laughed.

I shot a look of disgust in the general direction of the assailant. I dropped my bag and stood up. "Jack!" I shouted, running down the bleachers to the field.

"Back up. Give him some space," the coach instructed.

"Augh, coach. I'm hallucinating Andrea," Jack groaned.

"It's me you idiot," I sighed, relieved that he could speak.

"Keep your head in the game, Russell. Get up. That's all for today. The list will be in my office in a while," the coach announced.

Jack stood up and looked at me, his eyes were slightly unfocused. "Andie, am I really seeing you?"

"You are, Jack. You should go to the nurse. I think you might have a concussion," I fretted.

"Yeah. Thanks."

"Hey, Jack, you did well out there," I consoled.

"If I make the team, do you think Katie would go to the dance with me?" he asked innocently.

"It's worth a shot, Jack," I smiled without the heart to disappoint him.

I was on my way to the cafeteria for a quick lunch. Right before I walked in, someone grabbed my arm and pulled me aside.

"Wh-? Liam? What is it?" I asked, baffled.

"Your friend, Jack."

"What about him?" I asked, curious as to why Liam would mention Jack.

"You want him on the team, right?"

"I do," I confirmed.

"I could tell Coach that he can join. Coach likes him, you know. He made a point of telling me."

"Why would you let him on? What do you want?"

"For you to be my date to the dance this Friday."

"Why do you want me, Liam?"

"Well, you're cheer captain and I'm soccer captain. You're pretty and popular. Come on, Andrea, every girl in school wants to be my date. Why won't you agree to go with me?"

"Ohh," I said, rolling my eyes.

"Accept and I'll announce his name after cheer practice this afternoon."

I really wanted to see my best friend on the soccer team. He deserved it. This was my chance to help him.

"Fine, I'll go," I accepted.

"Great. I'll pick you up at 6:30. See you after practice."

He let go of my arm and I went into the cafeteria. I grabbed a lemonade before rushing to math class. Jack was already in his seat. The room was still empty, apart from the 2 of us. I sat on his desk and prodded his head gently.

"What did the nurse say?" I asked, concerned.

"I'm fine, Andie. You should go. Someone might see you talking to me," he replied desolately.

"So?" I demanded, not comprehending what he meant.

"The cheer captain shouldn't be talking to a nerdy soccer aspirant." I instantly caught up to his mood. Jack had an inferiority complex. It was expected, considering how Liam treated him. I always wished I could help him. I knew by experience that he would go into and come out of these moods on his own. I remained unhampered by his mood and pressed on.

"I don't care Jack. Lemonade? You should put something in that stomach of yours," I teased affectionately.

"Yeah. I'm famished," he admitted, meeting my eyes. I smiled knowingly and handed him my drink. He drank thirstily and handed me the empty plastic bottle. "I'll catch you later, Andie."

I could tell he needed some alone time, so I obliged. I slipped away from him silently as he put his head back down on the desk. I dropped the bottle in the recycling bin and took my seat.

After the final bell rang, I rushed into the girls' locker room. I changed into my cheerleading uniform. It was pretty generic. It was a cropped pink tank top with our school logo monogrammed on the front and a bright miniskirt. I grabbed my pom-poms – pink of course – and double knotted my sneakers. I rushed to the gym to find a handful of spectators, as usual. I easily spotted Jack. I adjusted the strap of my top to cover my birthmark before I started the session.

"Hey, everyone. Let's get started," I called in my perky cheerleader voice that Jack liked imitating. "Let's do some drills." We started stretching before moving on to more strenuous exercises. Practice went on for about an hour. "That's all for today ladies. I'll see you all tomorrow. Don't forget to find dates for the dance this weekend." It was my responsibility as the head of the dance committee to remind them.

"Hold on everyone," Liam intervened. Everyone looked at him expectantly. I was the only one who knew what he was going to say. "I have a very important announcement. As the captain of our soccer team, it's my responsibility to introduce you all to our players." There was a lot of buzzing chatter, people trying to guess who the lucky guy was. "I'd like to introduce the newest member of our soccer team..." he paused for suspense, savoring the moment. "Jackson Russell. Here's your jersey." I could tell he wanted to get this part over soon, he wasn't pleased that he had to address Jack.

"Wait, me?" Jack asked, surprise clouding his face. I could see the brightness in his eyes. I smiled to myself at that.

"Yeah man," Liam acknowledged reluctantly. I let it pass, he would realize how amazing Jack was soon. Liam threw Jack a number 7 jersey. Jack reflexively caught it as applause erupted around him. Jack instinctively pulled off his T-shirt and shoved the jersey over his head.

"I'm not done yet," Liam interrupted again. I was irritated at him for ruining Jack's moment of victory. The room quieted quickly. "I'd like to announce my date to the dance this weekend. You all know her. You all love her..." Again, he let the tension build. It was common knowledge that half of the girls in the room wanted Liam to pick them. He relished that fact. "Andrea Morgan."

Jack dropped his T-shirt and his mouth fell wide open. I would deal with him later. I had to arrange my face appropriately. I settled for a shy smile. All the cheerleaders clapped enthusiastically. It was ironic because I knew they all envied me. They would have given anything to be in my place. I was an exception and was immune to Liam's 'charms'. My idea of a good time on Friday night would be chilling in my room or Jack's, eating stale chips, and watching a movie.

Liam extended his arm to me. He was standing on the bleachers so people could have a better view of him. I contemplated for a few microseconds and took his hand. He pulled me up to stand next to him and I acknowledged all the watching eyes with another smile, blood rushing to my cheeks because of all the attention. This wasn't the kind of attention I wanted. I preferred flying through the air, performing a complicated cheerleading move.

"Thanks, guys," I murmured. "I have to go, but remember, I could still use volunteers to help with the dance." I twisted my hand out of Liam's, smiling formally again.

I could feel Jack's demanding eyes on me as I rushed out of the gym. I ignored them, for the time being. I could talk to him later. I had to get out of there before Liam could pull me back into the spotlight. I almost ran to the girls' locker room to grab my jacket. I pulled it on and went to the parking lot. Jack was waiting for me, as expected, leaning on his jeep. I threw my bag in the back seat and got in the passenger seat.

"Get in dude," I called after a minute.

"Liam?" he asked, indignant and full of disbelief.

"Ohh. Get in Jack. I'll fill you in."

He stuck his head in the window, not completely trusting that I would tell him.

"Spill," he demanded.

"Coach liked your talent, Jack. Liam was the only thing keeping you off the team. He said he'd let you on if I went to this weekend's dance with him."

He got in the jeep and started the engine. "You're kidding Andie," he said, still skeptical.

"I'm serious, Jack. Now that you're in and have your jersey, the coach will keep you on. Congratulations!" I said, with real emotion.

"Thanks," he blushed. I smiled gently at him.

"Just drive, Jack. We have a history test tomorrow," I was a little smug that I could give my best friend what he wanted.

Jack drove to his apartment and parked his jeep. We went directly to his room. His mom wasn't home yet. Jack pulled a textbook from his backpack and sat at his desk. I dawdled, leaning on the windowsill before condemning myself to my history revision. I fingered the curtains before pulling them back a few inches. I peeked out the window and down at the street that Jack's room looked into. My eyes widened as I caught sight of something a person wouldn't usually see in New York. I saw a large, grey, dog-like animal. It had big teeth – fangs – and was looking right at me. A wolf! That was impossible. People were walking right past it like it didn't exist. I shook my head, trying to make sense of what I was seeing.

"Andie, are you okay?"

"I thought I saw –" I looked out the window again and it was gone "– never mind."

I pulled the curtain closed.

"What's wrong?"

"I just hallucinated a wolf..." I said, letting my words trail off.

"A wolf in Brooklyn. That would be something," he said offhandedly.

Jack's dog plodded in and lay on the floor, his head raised in my direction. I scratched him absentmindedly and went to retrieve my book. I laid down on the bed and started reading.

Mrs. Russell came home a few hours later.

"Jack," she called.

"Coming, Mom," he replied and went out to the living room. He was back seconds later. "C'mon, Andie. Dinner."

I rolled off the bed and followed him out. This was normal, my dad and Mrs. Russell were never surprised to find us hanging out together. Jack pulled out a chair for me and I sat down.

"Hey, Andie," Mrs. Russell greeted warmly, "you like pizza, right?"

"Of course, Mrs. Russell," I replied.

"How was work, mom?" Jack asked.

"I didn't really have too much to do today. I did however hear some officers talking about a homicide out on Liberty Island."

"A homicide?" I asked, my mouth full.

"Yeah. A whole team is working on it. The victims are frozen."

"Hypothermia," I speculated out loud. I had heard my dad mentioning something like that before.

"No. They literally have ice on their bodies. I have no idea how they pulled that off. Ohh, Andie there's one more thing. Your dad is away for work. I'm not sure how long he'll be gone."

"Okay," I acknowledged. Dad's work took him all over the country. I tried not to be too disappointed.

"How was your day, kids?"

"I made the soccer team," Jack said, attempting to be nonchalant. I exchanged a look with his mom. We could see that he was bursting with excitement.

"That's great, Jack," she said, matching her tone to his. She hid a smile as he frowned at her. She surrendered and stood up. She hugged Jack and ruffled his hair. "I'm so proud of you, honey. Congratulations." She turned to me next, expecting an answer. She was like a mother to me too, I didn't think twice before answering.

"Nothing really eventful happened. I mean, I have a date to the dance."

"Ohh, are you finally dating?"

"No. He's not my type."

She seemed to understand I wouldn't say any more on the subject.

"Andie, do you need a ride home?" Jack asked after dinner.

"It's just a few blocks. I'll be fine, Jack, thanks."

"Nonsense. It's dark out and there is a potential killer on the loose. Jack, take Andie home safely." There was no further debate. Jack drove me home.

The next day, the whole school was buzzing about the homicide. I listened to the conversations but couldn't pick up much. I scheduled cheer practice at the same time as soccer practice and arranged for it to be on the soccer field.

"I'd love to go to the dance," Katie longed.

"I'm sure a bunch of guys have asked you," Sophia said, jealousy coloring her tone.

"I want a soccer player," she complained.

"I'm sure one of them will ask you," I reassured, making a mental note to tell Jack.

It was as if Jack was psychic. He approached us when he had a break from practice. He met my eyes before turning to Katie.

"Katie," he began, cautiously.

"Yeah," she said turning her profile in his direction.

"Hey. I don't know if you know me," he said as I internally cursed him for saying that. "I'm Jack. Will you go to the dance with me?"

"Sure. Why not. Pick me up at 6:15," she shrugged indifferently. I was a bit miffed at her attitude towards my best friend. Jack, however, was thrilled. He fist-pumped the air as Katie turned around.

I was happy for Jack but found myself distracted. I was thinking about the mysterious wolf I saw. There was something about it that unnerved me. It was looking right at me. That wasn't regular wolf behavior. Right?

2

The rest of the week passed in a blur. Between cheer practice and preparations for dance, I was exhausted. The mysterious homicides multiplied like rabbits. I knew, from experience, that it was only a matter of time before the FBI intervened, taking the case away from the local police. My dad was still away. I was hallucinating the strange wolf more frequently. It was on the school grounds, the alley next to my apartment, the streets, and even in the parking lot. Everywhere. It was as if the wolf was demanding my attention.

I was in my room, picking out an outfit for the dance. The door to my apartment opened and closed. I rushed out to the living room.

"Dad!" I rejoiced.

"Hey, sweetheart. I'm sorry I got called away on such short notice."

"I'm just glad you're back."

"I have to leave again in a few hours honey. Before that, I wanted to talk to you. Will you sit down for a couple of minutes?"

"Okay," I said, cautiously. My dad didn't usually orchestrate sit-down conversations.

"It's about your mom," he admitted. That immediately caught my attention. I loved hearing about my mom. I felt like I barely knew her, the woman who gave birth to me. She had died when I was 5 years old. I barely remembered her. Sometimes I dreamt of a gentle caress or a warm smile. I knew in my heart that it was her. I sat on the couch and he joined me.

"Andie, this may surprise you, but you're old enough to know. You have to know about what your mom left you."

"What do you mean Dad? What did she leave me?"

"She left you her entire legacy. I don't know much about it, but I'm sure you'll learn the rest soon enough."

"Okay," I said, curious this time.

"You have a brother," he stated. My jaw dropped in surprise. I couldn't believe it.

"I have a brother? Who? Where is he? Is he your son?" I demanded. I couldn't believe the words coming out of my dad's mouth. Whenever he spoke of my mom, he used a devout reverence. My brother had to be my dad's son. He was always clear about how much they loved each other. It was unnerving to imagine another man in her life.

"He's not mine. I'm your mom's second husband."

My jaw dropped in astonishment. I opened my mouth to protest.

"Andie hold on. Let me finish." He waited for me to shut up before he spoke again. "Your brother was 13 years old when your mom died. A while before she died, she told me about him. It was as if she knew that she was going to die soon. She told me that her son would protect his sister against anything if she ever needed it. If something ever happened to me, I want you to find him."

"How do I find him, Dad? I've never seen him before. Neither have you."

"I don't know. She told me that you would recognize him on sight. She also said that he would come find you if you needed him. I'm not sure what she meant, but I trusted your mother. I still do." He said this with such assurance that I couldn't help but believe him. I trusted my dad and I trusted his faith in my mother.

I needed some time to think about this, but I couldn't now. Liam would be here any minute and I was nowhere near ready. I wanted to cancel on Liam, but I couldn't put Jack's opportunity at risk. I decided to file this conversation away for later. "Okay, Dad. I have to go now. My date for tonight's dance is on his way."

He nodded and I fled to my room. I took a relaxing shower as I pushed the conversation as far away from my thoughts as possible. I couldn't let it distract me tonight. I dressed in a short-sleeved, dark blue dress that reached my thighs. I pulled on a pair of stylish boots and a black leather jacket. I let my hair down and brushed it out. I heard a knock on my door.

"Coming!" I called, walking out of my room with my phone. I opened the door and, as expected, Liam was waiting.

"Hey, Andrea, are you ready?"

"I am," I replied reluctantly, not feeling ready at all. Liam led me out to his car and I got in the passenger seat. All I could think about was how much more comfortable I would be if I was in Jack's jeep. He came by earlier to pick up my car, assuming Katie wouldn't want to ride in a jeep. My phone buzzed. It was Jack telling me that he had picked up Katie and was on the way to the school.

Liam pulled into the school parking lots and got out of his car. He opened my door and I got out, he determinedly took my hand and led me to the gym. The first thing I did was scan the room for Jack. I couldn't find him. I smiled to myself, assuming he was with Katie in some corner. About a half hour later, a slow song started. Liam pulled me close to his body, hands on my waist. I tried to shrug away. I wasn't comfortable having his hands on my body or being in such close proximity with him.

"C'mon, Andrea." He persistently pulled me closer. His grip was too strong for me to break. He tried to kiss me and I struggled to turn away.

"I said okay to the dance, Liam, nothing else. Let go of me," I ordered, keeping my voice firm.

Jack somehow pushed his way through the crowd and appeared next to me. He pulled Liam away from me. I could see the anger in his eyes. It was so chivalrous of him to stand up for me. Jack pulled his arm back, his hand curled in a fist and punched Liam. I realized I didn't need a brother when I had Jack.

"Didn't you hear her say no? Andie, are you okay?" I nodded at him, still in awe over his chivalry.

"Ohh, Russell, you're going to regret that. She said she'd be my date if I let you on the team. Don't you think I could pull you off easily?"

"I'm going to call your bluff. I know the coach likes me."

"Try me," Liam snarled.

"C'mon, Andie," Jack said, putting my jacket around my shoulders. I didn't know how he had it but I was thankful for the warmth. He pulled me out to the parking lot.

"He really might take you off the team, Jack."

"It's fine Andie," he shrugged.

"Where are we going?" I asked.

"To Central Park. It's still a beautiful night." I got in the passenger seat of my car and he drove to Manhattan. We found an empty bench in a dark corner of the park and Jack sat down. He patted the space next to him, inviting me to join him. I sat down and rested my head on his shoulder. His arm went around me automatically. I caught myself wishing that Jack was my brother. That I had a claim over him. I was staring out into the darkness and I saw the wolf again. I looked away, losing patience with my hallucinations. I glanced back again, knowing it would be gone. I was shocked to see that it was still there.

"Jack. Jack, look. There is it. The wolf I was talking about. It's right there."

"Andie, I don't see it," he said, concerned.

"Ohh, shut up," I dismissed, running to it. I was drawn to the wolf as it stared at me, its eyes intelligent. I was curious as to why I was the only one who could see it.

"Andie, hold on!" Jack called.

The wolf turned and padded into the trees. I followed it eagerly, leaving Jack trailing behind.

"Wait, where are you taking me?" I asked it. I didn't think I would be surprised if it spoke to me. It didn't. It led me to a huge clearing and lay down in front of a beautiful woman.

"We're not going to hurt you," the woman assured.

"Who are you?" I asked. I found myself close to trusting her, despite my best instincts. Some part of me told me that she wasn't lying.

"Good question," Jack said, winded.

Wolves appeared all around the woman. She seemed completely at ease in their midst.

"Who is the boy?" she demanded.

"My best friend, Jack."

"At ease," she addressed the wolves as if they could understand her. "We want to talk to you. Alone."

"Jack stays," I countered. I wasn't doing anything alone, no matter how curious I was to solve the mystery behind the wolves in New York.

"No, Andie, Jack doesn't stay. We both should go."

"Hold on, Jack. What do you want with me?" I asked, keeping an eye on Jack out of the corner of my eye.

"Attention. The alpha is coming," a man announced, winking at me. He was tall, and blond.

A second man walked into the clearing and took point, in front of the woman, shirtless. I caught a mark on his shoulder before he pulled a T-shirt over his head. He stood half in the dark.

"Are you sure it's her?" the woman asked, skeptically.

"Look at her," the blond said. I caught a hint of something else in his voice, appreciation maybe.

"I need to see your shoulder. Take off your jacket," the other man said.

"No," Jack protested.

"I'm not doing anything until you tell me who you are," I demanded. The man walked up to me, stepping into the moonlight, and held up a photo. It was a picture of my mom and me. I gasped and looked at him.

He was tall and tan. He had amber hair that looked like mine, with the absence of a black streak. He had emerald eyes that matched mine exactly.

"Let me see your shoulder," he asked again. This time I obliged. I pulled my jacket and sleeve aside, revealing my collarbone, shoulder, and birthmark. He moved the collar of his shirt until I could see the front of his shoulder. The mark on his shoulder was identical to mine.

"How?" Jack breathed in astonishment. I hadn't told him about my conversation with my dad.

"You're him. Lilian's son. My brother," I whispered into the night. I heard Jack gasp.

"I'm Ric. Alpha of the Eclipse pack. This is Celine and my second in command, Alex. I am Lilian's son."

3

"What alpha?" I demanded, the rest of the sentence not making any sense.

"We're werewolves," he stated simply as if that would explain everything. I resisted the urge to roll my eyes or drop my jaw.

"We?" I asked.

"Yes, we. It's nice to finally meet you, Andrea," he said, adoration and affection filling his words.

"Are you really my brother?" I asked incredulously.

"I am," he smiled.

"She's going to be alpha?" the woman named Celine asked dismissively.

"I'm what?" I demanded defensively.

"Andie, I think we should go," Jack suggested firmly.

"Andrea you're not going anywhere," Ric said, "There is still so much I have to tell you about our legacy. Our family."

"Look, it's dark. It's cold. Can we go talk somewhere else?"

"I suppose," Ric agreed reluctantly. He thought for a moment before saying, "Celine, you're in charge of the pack. Alex, get Eli, the jewelry and meet us at the house."

"What house?" I asked wondering where they were going to take me. I wanted to ask what jewelry they were talking about.

"Yours, Andrea."

"How do they know where my house is?" I asked.

"They know Andrea. Come, bring your friend."

"Jack," I called. He hurried to my side and put his arm protectively around me. Ric turned to Jack when we were back in the park.

"You will go home. Your home. I will take your friend home," Ric said in a no nonsense tone. I felt like he wasn't someone to oppose. I made a mental note not to get on his bad side.

"Andie?" Jack asked, analyzing my reaction.

"Sure Jack. Go ahead."

"Be careful. You better take care of her. I'll drop off your car," he promised and left.

"Andrea, wait here. When I return, get on my back. Don't be afraid." He went into the trees. I took a few seconds to compose myself. I couldn't believe it. I had a brother! I had always dreamt of having a brother. Someone to love me unconditionally. Someone to protect me. The moment I saw his shoulder, I believed him. There was no way he could fake the perfection in the birthmark. He was my mother's son.

A wolf came out of the trees with some clothes in his mouth. It was the wolf I had been seeing. It was bigger than I expected. It lay at my feet and met my eyes. I saw kindness and affection, safety and security, raw strength and power in his eyes.

"Get on," a voice in my head urged. I wasn't afraid. I put one leg over the wolf's back and he used his leg to help me pull myself up. I wrapped my arms around his neck. The wolf didn't move. I realized he was waiting for my approval to move. I ran my fingers through his fur.

"I'm ready," I assured. He started running. I felt like I was flying. He ran to the alley near my apartment and laid down again, letting me get off his back. He dropped the clothes and I watched in awe as he turned into a man. Ric got dressed and I led him upstairs. Alex and another man, Eli I assumed, were waiting at the door. I opened the door, letting them into my house.

"Sit down," I invited. They did and Ric started talking without hesitation.

"We are the direct descendants of the wolf god Fenrir and his sons, Hati and Skoll. We are descended from the daughter of Hati's son and Skoll's daughter."

"Fenrir, from Norse mythology?" I asked.

"Yes, Andrea. Our mother, Lilian, was one of the most powerful alphas of the Eclipse pack. Our pack is always led by a female alpha. I have been standing in for you since I was 13, leaving you to have a normal childhood."

"How are you so sure I'm one of you?"

"For starters, you are our mother's daughter."

"How does that make me one?"

"Did you hear a voice telling you to get on my back, in the park?"

"I did," I confirmed.

"That was me. A werewolf in his wolf form can send thoughts to other werewolves in human or wolf form. It proves you are a werewolf."

"I've never turned into a werewolf before," I protested. There was still so much that didn't make sense.

"That's because you didn't have the catalyst. I know you must have a lot of questions for me. This weekend is dedicated to teaching you, Andrea. You will be an amazing werewolf. I have been watching you all your life."

"I only started seeing you a week ago."

"I only let you see me a week ago, Andrea. Eli, the box." Eli was going to hand the box to Ric, who told him to give it to me directly. Eli gave me the box and I opened it.

"Don't touch it yet," Ric cautioned. "It's moonstone jewelry. You'll feel the wolf inside you when you touch it for the first time. Then, they'll help you control it, or rather, yourself."

He lifted the hem of his pants so I could see an ankle bracelet.

"Does my dad know about this?" I asked

"Mom said he did. My dad was human too. He died and I was raised by werewolves. Our mom gave us our birthmark. It is the sign of being part of the alpha's lineage."

"I barely know what I am. I don't know how to be an alpha," I admitted.

"You're a werewolf," Alex began. "We're proud, fierce and loyal. We are strong and protectors of the weak. We answer to your call, Andrea Velvela."

"It's Morgan," I corrected automatically.

"Mom's last name was Velvela. We carry her with us," Ric said, pride filling his voice.

"I barely knew her," I confessed.

"I did. We all did. She loved you so much," Ric consoled.

"I don't know that. Dad started field duty when I was 8. I've pretty much been on my own since then."

"Andrea, you were never alone. The wolves have always been with you. I was there whenever you were alone, protecting you, keeping an eye on you. I watched you learn how to ride a bike. I visited you in the hospital when you broke your arm cheerleading. I watched you get your driver's license."

All this overwhelmed me. I felt my head spinning.

"I'm tired," I said.

"Go to sleep Andrea," Ric suggested gently. "I know this is a lot to take in. Things will make more sense tomorrow. You won't be alone. Eli will stay outside your apartment. Tomorrow morning we train. The pack will join us."

I went to my room after I saw Ric out and shut the door. I showered, letting the warm water calm me. I ran the conversations over in my head, over and over again. This was my mom's legacy. That much was clear. I had to accept it. I wanted to know more about her. I wanted to know what she was like. I wanted to feel connected to her.

I had a brother. One who had been looking out for me all my life. He loved me unconditionally and would protect me. I wanted that. I would accept it. I decided to jump in with both feet, not bothering when I would resurface. I heard my phone ringing. I shut off the water and wrapped a towel around myself. I padded to my bed and answered it.

"Andie, are you okay?" Jack asked.

"Yeah, Jack. I was with my brother."

"I didn't know you had a brother."

"I only found out before the dance. Oh, speaking of the dance, what happened?"

"Well, Katie let me drive her to school because her car was in the garage. As soon as we entered the gym, she ran off."

"Jack, I'm so sorry."

"It's not your fault Andie. You couldn't have known what she would do. It's not important anymore. Tell me what happened. What did your brother say?"

"I'm a werewolf. Like my mother."

"And you believe that?" he asked.

"I do," I declared, looking at myself in the mirror, focusing on the undeniable proof on my shoulder.

I woke up the next morning and showered quickly. I dressed in jeans, a crop top, and a jacket. I ponytailed my hair and took the box of moonstone jewelry. I went out to the living room. I opened the door to my apartment and saw Eli and Alex waiting for me. I hoped they hadn't been waiting for too long.

"Hey, I hope you haven't been waiting for too long. Where's Ric?" I wondered out loud.

"He's with the pack. Are you ready to go?" Eli asked.

"Yeah," I grabbed a muffin and my car keys from under the doormat, where Jack left them last night. I led them to the underground parking and found my car. I got in the driver's seat and waited for them to join me. Eli got in the passenger seat.

"Alex?" I asked.

"I prefer to run. Meet me at Central Park."

I parked my car inconspicuously and Eli offered me his hand.

"Take my hand. You could get lost in the woods," he explained as I accepted his hand. He led me through the trees and back to the clearing we were in last night. There were more than 30 people, surrounded by wolves. Ric came through the trees on the other end of the clearing, wearing only a pair of shorts. His body had so many scars.

"Celine, the robe," he instructed. Celine brought me a bathrobe.

"Come with me," she invited. She led me through the trees again. "You need to change into this."

I did what she said quickly, in a hurry to get started. We went back to the clearing and Ric took the box of jewelry.

"Are you ready, Andrea? The moment the stones touch you, you'll feel the wolf. Let it consume you. Let it out. Let it roar. Let it empower you."

"I'm ready," I promised, without a trace of doubt. Celine, Alex, and Eli stood around me. Ric was in front of me.

"Wolves, ready," he commanded, alert. He took a necklace from the box and put it around my neck, I felt something shatter in me. It was like there was a wall holding back the wolf and it broke down. I started to shudder like I was being set on fire.

"Let it out," someone reminded. I embraced the fire for a moment and the next thing I knew, I was on all fours, surrounded by wolves.

"Easy. Calm, Andrea." Ric's voice said in my head. I whipped my head around. It was big and heavy.

"Andrea, it's Ric. Look at me." I tried to find the source of the voice. "Andrea, remember I told you we can communicate telepathically? Try it. Don't overthink it, Andrea. Be instinctive."

"How?" I thought instinctively.

"That's it. You did it. We all heard it," Alex's voice said.

"Only thoughts you want to share will be shared. You can focus it on just one wolf, with practice," Celine's voice informed.

"Andrea, the moonstones help you control the wolf. You can let it out or pull it back in," Eli thought.

"I'm freaking out here," I informed everyone. I felt overwhelmed again.

"The wolf won't hurt you. You are the wolf. Don't think of yourself and it as 2 different beings. Now you're going to go to the trees with Celine."

I willed myself to move and the most slender wolf followed me.

"Use the stones," Celine thought. "Use them to pull the wolf back."

I tried to imagine being human again. "I can't," I whimpered.

"Feel the wolf receding through your skin. Pull back your fur, then fangs, then stand up."

I willed myself to feel the wolf, to feel it being pulled back into my moonstones. The next thing I knew, I was human again. I was naked. Clean but off balance. My hair was loose. Celine threw me a fresh robe.

"Usually wolves tear down everything in their path the first time they transform. You did well," Celine appreciated.

We went back to the clearing.

"Andrea, you have a lot of control for a new wolf. The power of the alpha's blood coursing through your veins," Ric praised.

"Is that it? Are we done?" I hoped.

"Not by a long shot. That was the easiest thing you'll have to do all day."

"What about the clothes situation? I can't run around in a bathrobe." I couldn't run around naked either.

"We stash clothes all over the city. You should keep a change in your car, locker, and backpack too."

"Okay," I nodded. That was pretty straightforward. I should have thought of it myself. "What's next?"

"Not all the wolves you see around you are werewolves," Eli began. "But, we can control them. Celine sent one to lure you in last night. They are our brothers. They respect us. Every werewolf has a wolf that imprints on him or her. The wolf is smart and loyal. He'll protect you in your human form. Through him, you can communicate with other animals. Now, you have to let a wolf imprint on you."

"How do I do that?" I asked curiously. I wanted to do this right.

"Sit here," Alex said, pointing at a spot on the grass. I saw down and let the wolves surround me. I sat there until one of them put its head in my lap, staking a claim. The others, respecting that claim, backed away.

"Andrea, this is Orion," Ric said. "Go ahead, you can pet him." I scratched his head like I would do with a dog. His fur was shaggy and smooth.

"Hey, I'm Andrea," I introduced.

"He knows who you are, Andrea. His mother was our mom's wolf, Sif."

"Ohh," I said simply, taken by the majesty of all this.

"Take some time to familiarize yourself with him,"

"How? What do I do?"

"Take him for a walk in the park. People will think he's a dog."

"A walk? I'm in a bathrobe, Ric," I protested.

"That can be dealt with. Celine, give her some simple clothes."

Celine tossed me shorts and a T-shirt. I changed into them and Orion bounded back to me.

"What if I lose control?" I asked anxiously.

"Orion will help you. Remember, Andrea, he's not your pet. He's your equal."

I nodded. "C'mon, Orion."

We went to the park and wandered around aimlessly.

"Andie," a familiar voice called from behind me.

"Jack? What are you doing here?"

"You weren't at home. I assumed you'd be here."

"Ohh. What's up?"

"I should ask you that, Andie."

"I actually turned into a wolf, Jack," I declared, gushing a bit. I remembered what it felt like to be a wolf. I dropped down and found myself a wolf again.

"What?" I thought, perplexed.

"It's okay, Andrea. It's Orion. You can turn back in a minute. I'll get a robe for you."

I watched as Orion padded off. Jack's face was a mask of horror and shock. I approached him and nudged his leg.

"Andie?" he asked cautiously.

I nodded, it took me a second to realize how big I was. I was twice Orion's size. More like a bear than a wolf. My fur was amber, like my hair. Jack leaned down a little and touched my snout lightly. I licked his hand, trying to show him that I wouldn't hurt him. He laughed as my rough tongue tickled his palm.

Orion came back with some cloth and dropped it at Jack's feet.

"Am I supposed to pick that up?" Jack asked. I nodded encouragingly, meeting his eyes. He measured my look and picked it up.

"Turn back, Andrea," Orion thought. I focused on pulling the wolf back, I raised myself onto 2 legs and put my front paws on Jack's shoulders. I felt Jack cringe as my claws touched him. I felt the wolf recede and I was human again.

"It's me, Jack. Relax."

"You're naked," he noted uncomfortably.

"Ohh, sorry." I moved my hands off his shoulders instantly and he tossed me the robe. I pulled my hands through the sleeves and tied the belt around my waist. I smiled apologetically at Jack.

"Woah, Andie. That was..." he trailed off, at a loss for words.

"Freaky, I know," I agreed.

"Amazing, Andie. You were a wolf and it's broad daylight," he said enthusiastically.

"Thanks. Thanks, Orion. Jack, this is Orion. Orion, this is Jack, my best friend," I introduced,

Ric and Eli came barrelling through the trees,

"Andrea, are you okay? We heard your wolf thoughts," Eli probed.

"I'm okay. Orion helped me."

"Good boy, Orion," Ric praised. "What's the boy doing here?"

"I can't do this without Jack. Even if you don't let him stay, I'm going to tell him everything later. He's really smart and intuitive. He can probably help me."

"He can't tell anyone about this, Andrea."

"Hey, man, Andie's my best friend. I'd never do anything that would hurt her."

"I rest my case," I said smugly. "C'mon, Jack, we're going back to the woods." We followed Ric back to the clearing.

"What's next?" I asked eagerly.

"Sit down. I have to tell you about Heather and Wolfsbane." I sat down next to Ric and Jack sat on my other side. "They're both flowering plants that are dangerous to werewolves. Heather is toxic while Wolfsbane is lethal."

"What's the difference," Jack interrupted.

"Well, Heather would weaken you, but you would heal. If you get stuck with Wolfsbane you could die. You have to put vervain on the wound and then burn it out. Heather would just require stitches."

"Burn it out?" I asked.

"Yeah. It's the only thing that leaves scars." He took off his shirt and I looked at all the scars on his chest. "All these are wolfsbane scars. You can increase your tolerance to Wolfsbane with vervain pills. It'll give you enough time to burn it out."

"Umm... okay... vervain pills. Where do I get those?" I assumed I couldn't walk into a pharmacy and pick up a box.

"I'll give you some, Andrea. Take one every day." I nodded.

"Then there are your moonstones. Right now you're wearing a necklace. There are other articles in the box. You can use them according to what your day is going to be like. The ankle bracelet is easily concealed. The ring won't draw any attention. You don't need to wear moonstones to bed but you should have one item on you throughout the day. It'll automatically be hidden when you are in your wolf form and reappear in your human form. What I've given you now is for everyday wear. For formal wolf events, we have fancier articles. You'll see them soon. They are in the safe in our facility.

People won't see a wolf unless you want them to. You can project yourself as a dog or be invisible to all but one. If you want Jack to see you, he will. It's all in your mind Andrea. You need firm mental abilities. You need to believe you can do it and it'll happen. You can also pull out some parts of your wolf without transforming completely. You can have the claws or fangs or the eyes."

"What do the eyes do?" I wondered, interrupting his monologue.

"Your werewolf eyes glow amber. They detect heat and allow you to see in the dark."

"That is so cool," Jack commented.

"Jack, the only reason I'm letting you stay is so you can help her in places I can't," Ric explained.

"How do I do that?" he asked eagerly.

"The moonstones will help her stay in control but emotions trigger the wolf. The trigger differs from person to person. Emotions dominate cognitive control. Andrea may think she's in control but the emotion will make her transform. You have to be able to recognize the signs and be able to help her."

"What do I have to do?"

"You have to make her feel an equally opposing emotion or calm her down or just get her out of the public eye. It's usually a negative emotion."

"How do we find out what triggers me?" I asked.

"We'll test you against various emotions."

"How? Are you telling me that you're going to induce emotions in me?"

"We have a concoction that'll let me put scenarios in your brain. It'll wear off in a few hours."

"Okay, let's do it," I agreed.

"Celine, the syringe." Celine brought over a large syringe.

"Are you putting that in my arm?" I asked, my voice higher than usual.

"Your waist, actually. Look away."

I turned into Jack and held his arm. Ric put the needle in my body and I screamed, squeezing Jack's arm. "Ooh, Andie, that hurts!"

Ric took the needle out and I sighed. "It's not pain," I confirmed.

"You would have torn my arm off if you transformed," Jack said teasingly.

"We're wasting time. Let's begin."

"What should I do?" I asked.

"Just close your eyes. Let your mind wander."

I did and my mind was blank. I was suddenly running through New York City. My palms were sweaty and my breath was ragged. My heart pounded wildly against my ribs. I could tell I was being chased. I was running for my life. Fear.

My mind went blank again and the scene changed. I saw Liam picking on Jack. My muscles tightened and I felt heat rise to my cheeks. I inhaled deeply and marched up to Liam. I punched him in the jaw. I grabbed Jack and pulled him away. Anger.

Next, I was cheerleading. We were in a pyramid formation. I was on top. I knew what was going to happen next. The people under me would throw me and those on the floor would catch me. My heart raced again as I was thrown into the air. I smiled confidently and flipped mid-air. Excitement.

Then, I was lying on Jack's bed with his dog. We were sitting next to me. I was laughing at a joke he just told me. My breathing was even and my heart was calm. Pleasure.

My mind blanked again. "Open your eyes, Andrea," Ric instructed.

"What happened?" I asked.

"Nothing. Your heart didn't even react." I was confused. I remembered how my heart rate altered when I witnessed what Ric put in my mind.

"Then how else do we find my trigger?"

"It'll show itself in time. Now get dressed," he handed me my clothes. I went into the trees and got dressed. I went out, adjusting my jacket to cover my birthmark. It was a force of habit.

"You don't need to keep it covered. It's a sign of your ancestors and their legacy. Be proud of it, Andrea," Eli said.

"He's right," Ric said. I took off my jacket and hung it on my arm. "There's no way to teach you everything. You'll pick it up as we go, Andrea. Right now, stash clothes around the city."

"Alone? How do I know where to put them?"

"You can take Jack with you. Someone will give you a list of our stashes. Tomorrow, meet me at Brooklyn Bridge in the morning. There's something you have to see."

"Okay."

"Take Orion home with you. You don't need to lock him in. He'll always come back to you."

"What do I feed him?"

"Dog food is fine. He's perfectly trained. He might leave your house when you're at school. He might not also be home, but he'll be there when you need him."

"Sounds good. Jack, c'mon. Orion," I called. He bounded over to me. Eli gave me a paper listing the werewolf clothing stashes. Alex gave me a small box.

"These are vervain pills," he informed.

We went to my car. I waited for Orion to get into the back seat before getting in myself. I drove home. Jack was quiet the whole time.

"This is my place, Orion. Come on in. Jack, can I see you in my room?"

Sure, Andie... what's up?"

"Are you okay dude?" I asked, concerned by his silence.

"Yeah. I'm just wrapping my head around all this. You being a wolf. A long-lost brother. Royal mom."

"She wasn't exactly royalty,"

"She was alpha, right? That's basically werewolf royalty. You're werewolf royalty, Andrea." My mind strayed to being a wolf and I felt my claws pop out.

"Andie, claws," Jack noted. "What emotion were you feeling? The sooner we figure that out the better."

"Nothing. I was just thinking of being a wolf."

"So much for finding your trigger. Are you going to take off the stones tonight?"

"I do want to try. I'm not sure if I can do it tonight."

"Do you want me to stay over tonight?"

"Thanks for offering, Jack. I don't want to hurt you. I was going to ask Ric to join me."

"Sure." I took out a duffel bag and opened my closet. I stuffed in sets of clothes in it.

"Orion, Jack, and I are leaving," I informed. I was sure that he could understand me. I scratched him behind his ears before leaving. Jack took my bag and I went with him to my car. We checked off all the places on the list. I pulled up in front of Jack's apartment.

"I'll see you tomorrow, Andie," he waved. I took the paper Eli had given me and dialled the phone number scrawled across the top. It was labelled 'Ric'.

"Andrea, are you alright?"

"Yeah. I was wondering if you would stay over tonight."

"I'm outside the apartment. I'll be up in a minute."

"I'm on my way home. Orion's home. Let yourself in."

It took me a half hour to get home in the city traffic. I walked up to my apartment and threw my empty bag on the couch.

"Ric," I called, stopping in my tracks. I smelled something delicious.

"Hey, Andrea."

"What's that smell?"

"I'm making dinner."

"Ohh. It smells amazing," I complimented. "What's the occasion?"

"I thought we could eat and watch a movie. You know, brother-sister bonding."

"Sounds good. I'll join you in a few minutes." I showered and dressed in a tank top and shorts. I shook my hair out and went to the living room. I gasped at Ric's hair. It had a black streak like mine. I was sure it wasn't there before. I would have noticed. "Your hair," I breathed in awe.

"We can change one aspect of our appearance at a time. I'll teach you sometime," he said offhandedly. As if being to change how one looked was natural. "This is my natural hair. C'mon. No more wolf talk. You like pizza right?"

"Yeah," I agreed.

"I made a pizza. I did buy the dough though. I didn't have time to make it from scratch."

"Is it ready?"

"Yeah. I sat on the couch and he sat next to me, setting the tray between us. He poured me lemonade and put the glass on the coffee table.

"I'd prefer vodka," I smiled.

"You're seventeen."

"Doesn't matter. I've had vodka before," I protested.

"Fine. After dinner." He put on Romeo and Juliet.

"How did you know?" I asked, awestruck again. He had chosen my favorite movie.

"I know you've watched it hundreds of times. I heard it from the alley."

"Thanks," I said. After dinner, I got up to wash my hands. "It was delicious. You're a great cook."

"I learned to cook for you, Andrea. I always dreamed of this. Hanging out with you that is. I've longed for this since the day you were born. I was eight years old. I told Mom I'd always take care of you."

"You're doing a great job, Ric."

I got off the couch after the movie was over.

"Are you going to take off your moonstones?" he asked.

"I don't want to lose control," I admitted.

"You won't. The stones don't hold the wolf back. The moonstones are to help you feel the wolf after it has been awakened. When you first touched them, the wolf woke up. When you take them off, you won't feel the wolf in you, but it'll always be there."

"Okay. The guest room is down the hall. Help yourself."

"I'm fine on the couch, Andrea."

"Nonsense. Take a bed, Ric."

He smiled and left. I brushed my teeth and lay in bed. I took off my necklace and laid it on the bedside table. I closed my eyes and felt something on the bed next to me. I turned to see Orion.

"Hey, buddy. Good night," I whispered.

5

I woke up to knocking on my room door. "Mmm... I'm awake," I groaned.

"Andie, are you decent?"

"Mmm," I replied, rolling over.

The door opened and someone pulled the sheets over me.

"Andie, c'mon," Jack called I sat up and brushed the hair off my face. "Ric told me to ask you to get ready to go."

"Where's he?"

"Feeding Orion." I nodded and staggered out of bed and into the bathroom. I dressed in a spaghetti-sleeved, loose, knee-length dress. It wasn't something I would wear on the streets. I put on a braided belt, giving the dress some shape on my thin, curvy body. I untangled my hair and put on combat boots. I chose a moonstone ankle bracelet hidden under my boots and a ring. I put the box back in my dresser. I put a spare set of clothing in my backpack and went to the living room.

"What's with the dress?" Jack asked.

"I figured it'd be easy to take off when I turn. Ric, how come you don't have to wear a bathrobe?"

"That's because I'm, in complete control. I don't turn unless I want to. You'll get there, Andrea." I made myself a bowl of cereal.

"What are we doing today?" I asked as I ate.

"I have to show you something. It's past the bridge. I won't tell you now. I want to surprise you."

"Aren't we going to the park?"

"We're the werewolves of Brooklyn, not Manhattan," he said sarcastically.

We piled into Jack's jeep. "Be careful with her," he warned Ric, referring to his jeep.

"I'm a pretty good driver. Relax," Ric replied.

I got in the back seat with Jack while Orion was in the front seat. Rick drove to a spooky-looking dock.

"This is the Calvert Vaux Cove," Ric announced.

"Has it always been here? I wondered out loud. "I've been around here a million times." The place was mostly covered in a few inches of water. There was a dock on one side and the other shore was filled with a decent amount of trees. There was tall grass and mud all around.

"This is one of Brooklyn's abandoned places. No one comes here unless they mean to. We managed to construct our headquarters behind it. We have to go on foot from here. The garage is behind the dock. Someone will take care of your jeep, Jack. Be careful, Andrea. It's slippery. We had to make sure no one would accidentally find us."

Ric and Orion got out first. Jack got out and extended his hand to me.

"Andrea, you should come with me. Jack could fall himself."

"It's fine. I'll come with Jack." He might be my brother but I wasn't about to let him take my hand in less than 24 hours of our meeting. I gripped Jack's arm securely and got out of the jeep. Ric led us to a building that looked abandoned. It was around half a mile behind the shore. Trees surrounded it. The building looked ancient and rundown.

"This is it?" I asked, trying to hide my disappointment.

"You should see the inside," he laughed, reading my disappointment. I wasn't sure I wanted to see the inside if the outside was this bad.

"Are you sure it's safe?" I asked quizzically.

"See for yourself. Jack, hold on. Only people with moonstones can enter and see it for what it is." Ric pressed a simple moonstone ring into Jack's hands. "Put it on. It won't hurt you." Jack slipped it on his third finger and we entered the structure. My jaw dropped.

The building looked completely different on the inside. It was a beautiful structure. It looked like it was filled with the most sophisticated cutting-edge technology. I was scared to touch anything, worried it was just a dream and that my touch would make everything disappear. I inhaled and I could almost taste the expensive materials used to construct this magnificent facility.

"Andrea, welcome to the Eclipse facility. We have an artifact that makes the building look abandoned from the outside. It makes sure no one who isn't supposed to be here gets in."

"It's beautiful," were the only words I could form.

"We're way more civilized than you think," Eli teased, coming up to us. "We can access all of the city's cameras and official records from here. We have state-of-the-art training and residential quarters. Most of us live here.

So do the wolves. They have their own quarters."

"Andrea, I want to show you something. Jack, don't get lost," Ric warned. I followed him up a couple flights of stairs, to a room filled with portraits.

"This room is called Alpha Hall. Each of our pack's alphas are in this hall. This one in the center is Arcadia, the daughter of Hati's son and Skoll's daughter. She was our first alpha. It's because of her that we are matriarchal." Arcadia was undoubtedly beautiful. She had dark brown hair that was choppy and flowy at the same time. She had sharp emerald eyes that wouldn't miss anything. Her long limbs seemed fluid, even in stillness. She wore a simple dress, but was ethereal.

"This is our mother," he pointed out to me. It was a portrait of a maternal looking woman. She looked a lot like me, but more like Ric.

"This is where your picture will be," he declared, pointing to an empty frame next to her picture.

"Are you sure I'll be on here?" I asked, filled with uncertainty.

"Of course. You are our mother's daughter. Come on." He led me out of the hall to another aesthetic room. It had a desk and a plush chair on one side of the table. There were two more chairs on the other side. There was a small couch on the other end of the room. The table had a laptop and a few books. There were bookshelves on one of the walls. The rest of the walls were filled with pictures. I was surprised to see my face on a lot of them. "This is my office. Or rather, the alpha's office."

"It's great. Everything is great."

Ric seemed to sense my tension. "Hey, don't worry. Relax. Do you want to do some physical wolf stuff?"

"Sure," I agreed.

"We'll do some hand-to-hand combat." We went to the training area. Ric pulled me onto the sparring mat.

"As a werewolf, you have strength, super senses, and fast reflexes. Now use them." I wasn't sure how to use them but I resigned myself to trying. I took off my shoes and stood steadily – or so I thought – on the mat. "Keep your hands up. Cover your face." We started sparring and he kicked my waist with the front of his foot in 2 seconds. I fell, not expecting such a strong touch. "Your oppressors won't go easy on you. Try to dodge. Guess my moves. Trust your instincts," he instructed.

We sparred for a few hours. I couldn't stay up for more than 5 minutes. Jack and Celine stood by, watching.

"I thought she'd have gotten you by now, Ric," Celine said.

"Thanks," I replied, sarcastically.

"No one but my mom has ever taken me down hand to hand. You know that, Celine."

"She's Lilian's daughter. You know that," she retorted quickly.

"And I'm her son," Ric contradicted quickly.

I inhaled and went for Ric. He easily caught me in a death hold. I exhaled and bent over forward using my arms and back to throw Ric over my shoulder, keeping pressure in my stomach. Ric's back was on the mat. I knelt with my knee on his chest and my forearm across his neck.

"Your sister, Lilian's daughter, took you down," I smiled, triumphant.

He moved like lightning, grabbing my waist. He flipped me over his head onto my back.

"I don't think so. In your defense, that was amazing for someone who has never fought before."

"Ric, everyone's ready," Celine said impatiently.

"Andrea, go with Celine to clean up and come back down. There are some people you have to meet."

"Follow me," Celine invited. She led me to a room on the 4th floor. "These are my quarters. Come in. Go wash your face and brush your hair."

"Why? What's going on?" I asked, confused.

"Ric's going to show you off to the elders and the pack. You have to change your clothes as well."

"Change?" I asked again.

"Absolutely. Look at me." I did. She was in a deep-necked leather dress with cut-outs. "You can borrow one of my dresses." I noticed her cradling her stomach. I didn't notice yesterday, but she looked pregnant. Her stomach strained against her beautiful dress.

"Umm..." I began indecisively, about to ask her about her pregnancy. She threw me a dress. I changed into it a few minutes later. It was black leather, backless and short. It was held up by a strap around my neck. I shook out my hair and put on my boots.

"Is your birthmark showing?" she demanded.

"Yeah," I confirmed.

"Good. Come." Celine led me downstairs where Ric was waiting outside a door. He was in jeans and flannel.

"I see you got her into a dress, Celine. Andrea, Celine is very comfortable with her body. You don't need to be just like her."

"Are you telling me that I could have stayed in my own outfit?" I demanded.

"Where's the fun in that?" Celine said with a mock pout. Ric extended his arm to me and I took it without hesitation now.

"Allow me to present you, Ms. Morgan," he requested. Celine held the door open for us. Ric walked me to a raised platform in the room. "Can I have everyone's attention...?" Ric called. "I'd like to introduce my sister, Lilian Velvela's daughter, Andrea Morgan."

"Is she really the child we have been waiting for?" one old woman asked.

"Yes, Ms. Kenner."

"She better be able to avenge Lily's murder."

"Murder? No. She had cancer," I corrected

"No dear. She was murdered," the woman pressed.

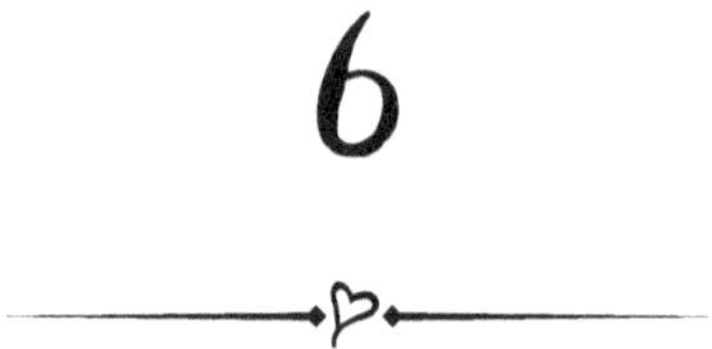

"That'll be all. Andrea will be here all day," Ric intervened. Alex and Eli appeared in front of us and let Ric herd me away. I couldn't think straight. The story I'd been told my whole life was a lie. I was led into a room, probably Ric's. I vaguely noticed Jack in front of me.

"Andrea, let me explain. Listen to me. Our mom was killed by the Dokkalfar." He hurried to explain things to me.

"Am I supposed to know what Dokkalfar are?" I demanded, too terse to care about how rude I was being.

"They are dark elves," he said hurriedly. "Creatures of the night. They waged war against us, here in New York. Our mother was our supreme commander during the war. She was captured and executed during the war. They didn't even give us her body. She should have been buried in our graveyard, with our ancestors," he lamented.

"Why did they wage a war?" I asked, genuinely curious now.

"The Dokkalfar are our natural enemies. Our territories have always bordered each other. They've always wanted to expand their territories. They wanted control of New York and the surrounding areas. But, we weren't going to give up our city. I went into battle at thirteen. We drove them out of the city."

"How could you fight at thirteen?"

"I was raised here, Andrea. I started training as soon as I could walk."

"What happened to the dark elves?"

"They're still out there somewhere. They haven't attacked us again. At least not yet. We have hostages."

"What do you mean? Did u capture a soldier?"

"We took three of their children. They are in the most secure part of this building. Do you want to see them?" he offered hesitantly. I could tell he hoped I would refuse.

"Alright," I agreed.

"You should know, they're all grown up now."

"Take me to see them," I demanded, standing up. Ric and Alex exchanged looks.

"Come with us. Jack stay here with Celine."

Ric led me to the basement level with a sword someone had handed him. Eli and Alex followed us with their claws out. "Andrea stay alert. Don't touch the barrier. It's highly electric and could put you in a coma."

"What barrier?" I asked, confused. I couldn't see any barriers in the room.

"It's invisible. Stay behind me and hold this." He gave me a flashlight. Something darted in front of us. I caught a flash of red. I stepped forward, shining light around the room. Ric took my arm and pulled me back. He pointed his flashlight to the ceiling. I saw a metal-like device on the roof of the room. "That's the device that projects the barrier."

"Where are they?"

"That was them." Eli and Alex used their flashlights to herd them together so I could see. They were pale white and had bright red eyes. They had elfish eyes and wrinkly skin. "Fire could kill them and they're sensitive to light."

I lost my focus and I found myself on all fours. I looked up at Ric. I was a wolf again.

"It's okay, Andrea. You're still learning. Come on up. Let's use this as a chance for you to learn something else." He led me to the training area. "Andrea, try to make yourself invisible. Eli, transform and help her." I averted my eyes as Eli stripped and turned into a wolf.

"Remember, it's all in your head," he thought at me.

"Am I just supposed to imagine no one can see me?" I thought.

"Hold that thought. Every single wolf can hear you. Let's work on that first. It's just like talking. Talk to Ric."

"He's not a wolf now," I stated.

"When you're a wolf, you can send your thoughts to members of the pack who are in their human form. Imagine you're telling him a secret," Eli encouraged.

It took me an hour to get the hang of it. Until then, I heard exasperated sighs all around me.

"Andrea, you did it. I couldn't hear what you said," Eli congratulated. "Now, include me in your line of thought."

"Can you hear me?" I thought. Eli and Ric nodded. Celine came down with Ric.

"Why is she a wolf? What happened to my dress?" Celine demanded.

"I'll get you a new dress, Lay her off," Ric said. "Andrea, turn back."

"What about my clothes?" I thought.

"Nudity is an unavoidable part of being a werewolf. Don't overthink it." Ric held up a fresh dress. I focused on pulling the wolf back through my moonstones. I was back on two legs and I quickly pulled the dress on.

"I'm sorry about the dress," I apologized.

"Don't worry. I was just teasing. I've shredded my fair share of clothes," Celine smiled.

A majestic wolf approached Ric. "Hey, girl. Andrea this is Hope, my wolf. Hope, love, my sister, Andrea."

"Love?" I asked, wondering why he would refer to his wolf that way.

"Yeah," he said absentmindedly, listening to what Hope was telling him. "What is it, girl...? I'm on my way. Alex, go check in with the cops. Eli, fortify the facility. Celine, the basements. Andrea, stay with me."

"Ric, what's wrong?" Celine asked.

"Dokkalfar in Boston. They wouldn't dare come back here, but we can't be too careful. I don't want you to leave my side, Andrea. Hope, guard her" Ric rushed to the main room and I followed with Jack in tow.

"Jack's mom is a cop. He can help," I suggested.

"Fine. Jack go with Alex." Jack rushed off and Ric was observing the screens.

"What do you see?" I asked.

"I'm hoping I don't see anything. We have cameras all over New York. I don't want to see them here."

"How do you know they're in Boston?"

"We have people in the FBI. They got a case about icy homicides. Dokkalfar have power over ice."

I felt like I'd heard something like that before, but I couldn't place it. "What can I do to help?" I asked eagerly.

"Right now, training. You can't do anything unless you can protect yourself. Just because you're a werewolf, doesn't mean you don't need to learn how to use weapons. You need to have them on you at all times. They'll conceal themselves when you're not using them. The moonstones will hide them. When you are in cheer practice, wear the moonstone ring. If you twist the stone, a tiny blade will pop out. It'll give you enough time to get your weapons. Hold on for a second... Lise, come watch the monitors," he instructed. "Hope stay here... Andrea, come on."

"Where?" I asked. I assumed we would be staying here.

"To pick your weapons. You will be using a bunch of assorted weapons, but there will be one or two that are best suited to you."

"I don't get why a werewolf needs weapons," I protested.

"Look, the wolf provides us with resilience and strength and endurance. But, we don't usually fight in our wolf forms. Most of our enemies can't be taken down by a wolf's fangs or claws. They'll help."

"If you say so," I agreed amicably.

He led me to a room full of weapons; knives, swords, blades, daggers, bows, arrows, daggers, spears and various unknowns.

"Try one," he encouraged.

"Umm… you realize I'm a seventeen-year-old New York teenager. I have no idea how to use these." Ric laughed and took a sword off the racks.

"This should feel balanced. Here." I gingerly took the sword. "Hold it steady, Andrea. It won't bite." I held the hilt as he knelt in front of me. He eased off my boots and put two leather straps around my calves. "These will hold four blades each. I'll show you how to put them in, later. The blades have leather sheaths so they don't hurt you. Your boots will cover them."

Then, he put two straps on my upper arms. "These can hold longer blades."

"Ric, do I really need all of this?" I asked, putting the sword down.

"You need at least one of these on your body at all times." He took another strap and put it around my waist. "This is a scabbard. You can wear a belt with jeans and stick your sword in it. You could also hide it under a short skirt or conceal it in a long one."

"Umm, okay," I agreed, unsure what else to say.

"Andrea, I don't want to come off as overprotective. It's just that you don't know what's out there yet."

"I get it, Ric."

He pulled out a few chests. "There are different sizes of blades. Take them and put them in the straps." I knelt and filled my blade holsters.

"Am I doing it right?"

"You're doing wonderfully, Andrea. Come, pick your sword."

"How do I know which one?"

"I'll lead you to them. Close your eyes and pick one. That will do for now. Once you know more, you can pick a different one if you want to." I closed my eyes and let Ric lead me forward. "Reach forward." I did and wrapped my fingers around the first hilt I felt. I opened my eyes.

"Is this okay?" I asked.

"It's perfectly balanced and will do great in battle."

"What battle?"

"Whichever one comes next. You can take off your weapons. I'll have them packed." I carefully took off the leather and laid them on the table. "Let me show you to your room," he offered, taking my sword in hand.

"Ric, this is all great, but you should know, I'm not staying here. I have a place of my own."

"I know, Andrea. It's for when you hang out here, after school."

"Okay, Let's go." He led me upstairs and into a room every bit as beautiful as Celine's. "Mom picked this room for you years ago. It's been waiting for you. Celine stocked your closet yesterday."

"Celine?" I asked warily.

"Mmhmm. I know I said you could wear your own dress, but werewolf girls usually wear dresses like Celine's. They are very comfortable with their bodies like Celine is. It was a good thing that she got you into that dress. It made a good first impression on the elders. I know you haven't seen a lot of female wolves here. Some are mothers and are home today. Others have steady jobs. Others are in college dorms or are patrolling the city."

"Are you telling me that all werewolf girls dress like Celine?"

"Most of them do. Sometimes they wear clothes that are more revealing. I made sure Celine toned it down a bit when she was stocking your closet. I guess it's easier for them to turn."

"If you say so. I'll take some home with me."

"Sure, Andrea." I turned to look in my closet when the door of my room burst open.

"Sorry," a man said hurriedly. "Ric, Celine's fainted."

"Wasn't she guarding the Dokkalfar?" I asked.

"Yeah," Ric replied absently, sprinting out.

"Where's he going?" I asked the man.

"Infirmary. Celine is eight months pregnant."

"What?" I knew she was pregnant but I didn't realize she was so far along.

"Follow me. I'll take you to them." I followed the man to the infirmary.

"Celine, are you okay?" I asked when I saw her on a bed.

"I'm fine, Andrea. Ric, relax," she said taking his hand. The way she looked at him made me wondering about the relationship they had with each other. He was on his knees, on the floor next to Celine's head. I expected him to be comforting her, but here she was, with her palm on his cheek. She was looking at him with comforting eyes, soothing him.

"I shouldn't have put you on duty so close to labor," he regretted.

"Ric, go. I'll be fine. You have other responsibilities," Celine urged.

"Who's the father?" I asked curiously.

"She'll never tell us. Celine, call me if you need anything. Andrea, stay with her for a little while." He put my sword on the table and left with the other man. I sat on a chair next to Celine's head.

"Ric and I dated," she explained.

"That's why he's so worried. Is the baby his?"

"No. She'll never meet her father."

"Why not?" I asked, confused.

"It was a one-night stand, Andrea."

"Ohh. That makes sense."

"You look so much like Lilian," she reminisced. "I was abandoned as a baby. Lilian found me and treated me like a daughter. She turned me."

"Turned you?" I asked.

"I wasn't born a werewolf like you or Ric. Lilian bit me on a full moon and I became a werewolf. We're most powerful during the full moon. Those are the only days we can turn humans into werewolves. We are also most volatile during the full moon."

"I feel like everyone other than me knew my mom," I lamented.

"She loved you and lives on in you. I was the first to hold you when you were born. I was five years old. I was so excited to have a sister. We didn't know she would raise you as a human."

"What was it like to grow up with werewolves?" I asked curiously.

"It was amazing. It was like being surrounded by a huge family. Alex and Eli were like brothers to me. Ric was with Lilian all the time, preparing to be alpha. We didn't know where you were or when she'd bring you back, so Ric took the responsibility. That's all I want for my little wolf. A loving family. People who'll fight for her."

"What about you and Ric? Are you still into him?"

"Of course. I always have been."

"He looks like he likes you too. What happened?"

"He thinks loving him will put me in danger. It got worse when I got pregnant. I was at a bar after the breakup and got drunk. I slept with a random guy and I found out I was having a baby."

"That's nonsense," I dismissed, referring to my brother's attitude.

"I wish he was her dad," she admitted. "Never mind that. How is your training going?"

"I'm not sure. I think I'm doing well."

"Is that your sword?" she asked, I heard an undertone of something in her voice. I wasn't sure what.

"Yeah," I confirmed.

There was a knock on the door. "Come in," she invited before I could press the matter. Alex and Eli came in.

"Hey, are you okay?" Alex asked.

"I'm fine guys," she reassured.

"Is Jack with you?" I asked.

"He's downstairs," Eli said. I took my sword and ran downstairs.

"Andie," Jack called when I saw him. I hugged him tightly. "Are you okay?" he demanded, worry coloring his tone.

"I'm fine, Jack. I'm just a little sentimental right now. What happened? What did you find?"

"I'm not sure," he admitted.

"Andrea!" Ric's voice came.

I went to him and Jack followed me. "Who's with Celine?" I asked.

"Alex and Eli," he answered.

"Jack, go find them. They're on the second-floor infirmary." I waited for him to leave. "Ric, can I tell you something."

"Of course,"

"It's about Celine. She is still so into you. I can tell you're into her too." I was so sure that they would be perfect for each other.

"She's about to have a baby. It could be any day now. It's not safe for me to be with her."

"You said no one has ever defeated you in combat. You could protect her and her daughter. You both would be so much happier."

"We were happy, Andrea. All I want is for that little girl to be safe and healthy."

"She will be, Ric."

The others came down and joined us before I could press the matter anymore. "Celine, sit down," Ric instructed firmly. "Guys, report."

"The facility is secure," Eli began. "All guards are up."

"There's nothing in the city, according to the FBI. They'll let us know if anything shows up," Alex informed.

"Okay. We'll set up a 24/7 rotation. Celine, all you're going to do it take it easy. Andrea, –"

"– I have to get home. I have a math quiz tomorrow," I stated, realizing how mundane that sounded.

"You're going home? Dokkalfar could be anywhere."

"Dad could come home. I need to talk to him about all this."

"You can't be alone. I have to be here tonight. I can't stay with you."

"I'll go with her," Celine said.

"You should be taking it easy," Ric protested.

"I can still take care of Andrea," she said.

"Fine, Eli take the case," Ric said. Eli brought over a large briefcase. "Andrea, these are your weapons and the straps." He took another long box. "This is for your sword."

"I got it, Ric," I said.

"Celine, come back here in the morning. Andrea, be careful in school." Jack, Celine and I went to the jeep and Eli followed with the weapons and a bag of clothes. I didn't want to admit it yet, but, I was sure I'd be comfortable in the clothes Celine put in my closet. I was pretty comfortable with my body. I waited for Celine to get in the back of the jeep and got in the front. Eli gave me the bags.

"Hey, Andrea," he began.

"Yeah?" I asked curiously.

"Do you want to go out tomorrow?" he asked carefully.

"With you?" I confirmed.

"Umm...Yeah," he said shyly.

"Sure. Why not?"

"Great, I'll pick you up after school. We can catch a movie."

"Okay," I smiled.

"I'll come pick you up tomorrow, Andrea."

I nodded and led Celine up to my apartment. "I'm exhausted. What about you?" I asked.

"So am I," she agreed.

"This is the guest room. Make yourself comfortable. You probably will be. Ric slept there last night," I teased. She laughed at me. "There's food in the refrigerator. Do you want a change of clothes?"

"Thanks," she accepted. I gave her a loose T-shirt and shorts. "Good night, Andrea."

Chapter 7

I walked out of my room the next morning in a low-cut, full-sleeved top and jeans. I had a moonstone necklace and a strap around my calf with a blade concealed in my boots. Celine was sitting on the couch.

"Did you sleep well?" I asked.

"Yes. Thank you," she replied.

"Do you want some breakfast?" I asked.

"I'll eat at the facility." Right on cue there was a knock on the door. I let Jack in.

"What's with the clothes, Andie?" I have to admit, I did look amazing in my fitted outfit.

"It's a wolf thing. Celine, lock the door on your way out and put the keys under the doormat."

Jack and I got into his jeep.

"How do you feel, Andie?" Jack asked concerned.

"I'm really nervous," I admitted. I don't want to lose control in class."

"Hey, listen. I won't leave your side," he promised.

"I don't want to hurt you, Jack. You're my best friend."

"That's exactly why you won't hurt me," he declared confidently. "I won't let you lose control. Your brother will probably be around somewhere."

"You have to make sure I stay calm," I instructed.

"I will, Andie. Hey, do you have a weapon on you?" he asked suddenly.

"I have a blade in my boots and these," I said, flashing my claws.

"Okay, those are terrifying," he accepted. His eyes widened as he observed my claws.

"I'm putting a set of clothes in here in case you need to bring them to me," I informed, referring to the jeep.

"Sure," he agreed instantly. He parked at school and we got out of the jeep. He hesitated before starting to walk to class.

"What's wrong, Jack?" I asked. He shook his head and squared his shoulders. "Ohh, Jack. I'm so sorry. I forgot about Liam and the dance and the team," I apologized.

"We have bigger things to think about, Andie. Come on." I was extremely tense as we went to our first class. Jack sat in front of me as Liam and Oliver walked in.

"Hey, Morgan, Russell," Liam began. "Did you guys do anything interesting on Friday night?" I knew exactly what he meant when he asked me that.

My claws popped out in anger. I could see Jack reacting as well. He stood up before I could stop him. Jack punched Liam as the teacher walked in. I felt fangs tearing into my lips. "Russell, it's on," he threatened. I clutched the desk tightly, my claws forming impressions in the wood.

"Thank you, boys, sit down," the teacher said.

"Jack," I hissed. He turned, surprised by my tone, and saw me losing control. He knelt in front of my desk, hiding my face from view.

"Andie, Andie. Andie, it's okay. I'm okay. Calm down. They're just some jerks. Look at me. It's Jack..." he whispered hurriedly.

"Mr. Russell," the teacher called impatiently. Jack gently pried my fingers off the desk and held my hands in his.

"Yeah, hold on," he replied off-handedly. He looked into my eyes and I forced myself to concentrate. "Andie, focus. Use the moonstones," he urged. I inhaled, pulling back my claws and fangs as I breathed. "Are you okay? Do you need to leave?"

"I'm calm," I assured.

He nodded at me, not letting his eyes stray away from mine. He squeezed my hand lightly and took my seat. "Ms. Morgan, do you need to be excused?" the teacher asked.

"I'm fine."

"Okay. Boys, I don't want any funny business in my class." After class, I was leaning on my locker and Jack was next to me.

"I thought anger didn't trigger you," Jack remembered.

"It's not anger, Jack. I just hate people treating you like that. You have to nail this Friday's game."

"I will, now go lead your team," he encouraged. I had cheer practice now. "I'll see you at soccer practice later."

I changed into my uniform and took off my blades. I put on my ring as Ric advised. I double-knotted my sneakers and went to the gym. "Hey, girls.

Today we're going to challenge ourselves. I want to see your best moves." In reality, I wanted to see what I could do with my new reflexes. I wanted to see how agile I was. I stretched and jumped.

I flew into the air and flipped thrice. I landed on my toes. I leaned back until my hands touched the ground. I kicked into a handstand. I used my arms to push myself into the air again. I did a backflip and landed on my arms again. I moved my legs so I could stand again.

I looked around the room. Everyone was watching me. "Woah girl, that's why you're captain," Alisson praised.

"Thanks," I acknowledged.

"How did you pull that off?" she pressed.

"I've been practicing," I lied smoothly. It was easy for me to pull off those moves. I wondered what I could do if I tried hard. After practice, I rushed to the locker room. I traded my sneakers for boots and stuck my blade in. I stayed in my cheer uniform. I ponytailed my hair and went out to the bleachers. I crossed one leg over the other as I sat in the front. Jack came out in his jersey. He smiled at me and I smiled back. Liam and Oliver bumped Jack as they ran onto the field.

About fifteen minutes later, a ball came hurtling towards me. I lifted my leg and kicked the ball in mid-air, toward the goal. I watched it go into the net and turned my focus back to Jack.

"You! Cheerleader! Get over here!" the coach called.

"Me?" I asked, confused.

"Yeah!" he replied. I crossed over to him and the team gathered around. "Do you play soccer?" the coach asked.

"Not really," I shrugged.

"Well, congratulations! You just made the team," he informed me coolly.

"What?" I asked, baffled.

"That was a goal."

"I'm Andrea Morgan, captain of the cheer team," I protested.

"I don't care. You have to be on the team." I looked at Jack who was next to me. He nodded at me, smiling.

"Coach, are you kidding me right now? A girl on the soccer team?" Liam exploded.

"Being a girl doesn't matter. Talent does. This girl definitely has some," the coach announced in a no-nonsense voice.

"Coach, if I accept, Jack is on the team for good," I countered.

"I can live with that," he agreed.

"I can't," Liam interrupted. I felt my anger spike and my claws appeared.

"I'm in," I accepted.

"Congratulations," the coach repeated.

"Oh my god. Morgan's a girl and Russell is a freaking nerd," Liam protested. I couldn't control myself. Jack put his arm around me to calm me.

"Excuse me, coach," I muttered. I pushed Jack away, with more force than I intended and ran towards the building.

"Go get the girl some gear, Russell," I heard the coach instruct. I threw the doors of the building open and kicked off my boots. I shut the door of the girls' locker room and ripped off my clothes. I let the wolf out. It wanted to roar. I growled and my paw turned on the shower. I heard voices in my head.

"Andrea, it's Ric. You need to calm down. We can't get in the school. Take deep breaths. We'll talk about it later. Breathe with me." I focused on his breathing and matched mine to his. I turned human again. I heard the door open and close.

"Andie, it's me," Jack informed.

"Can you grab a towel?" I asked. He threw me one and I secured it under my arms.

"Can I look now?" Jack asked a minute later.

"Yeah," I agreed. He poked his head around the lockers and walked to me.

"Hey, Andie. Are you okay?" he asked. I nodded at him. "I got your shoes. Oh, this is your jersey. I also got your clothes from the jeep." He started handing me my clothes.

"Jack, you're a lifesaver," I cherished.

"I'll let you get dressed. I'll be right there." I pulled on my shorts and the jersey as he went behind the lockers again. I used a hair tie to pull the jersey to one side. I went to Jack and hugged him. He winced and I let go immediately.

"What's wrong?" I demanded.

"It's nothing. I'm fine," he soothed.

"Shut up and take off your shirt," I commanded. He shook his head and my fingers went to the hem of his jersey. There was nothing romantic in the movement. I had seen Jack topless so many times that I was desensitized to it. "Jack, c'mon," he raised his arms and let me pull his jersey off. The first thing I registered was that his jersey was torn. I'd ripped through the fabric with my claws. I put my hands on his shoulders and turned him around so I could see his back. My heart skipped a beat. He had gashes on his back.

"Ohh my god Jack. Did I do this?" I asked, horrified.

"It's fine. I know what I signed up for, Andie."

"Where else did I get you?" he held out his arm and I saw a single scratch on it. I covered my mouth with my palm as tears welled up in my eyes. I was horrified.

"Hey, Andie, don't worry," he soothed. He pulled me close to him and I rested my cheek on his bare chest. I felt bad that he was soothing me when he was the one who was hurt. I pulled away after a moment and brought over a first aid kit. I took out some antiseptic cream and gently applied it to his arm. He wrapped a bandage around it.

"Let me help with your back," I offered. He nodded and lay face down on the bench. I used gauze to clean his back and put on a bandage.

"We have to get back to the field," Jack said. He put on a fresh jersey and stood up. I put on my sneakers and went out with Jack.

"Ahh, Russell, Morgan, glad you could finally join us," the coach said sarcastically.

"Sorry coach, I felt like I was going to throw up," I apologized.

"Well, go get in there. Russell, cover her," the coach ordered.

"Coach, I think she could cover me better." Jack looked uncertain when the coach stared him down.

"Shut up, Jack. C'mon."

I walked into the cafeteria after practice and noticed everyone's eyes on me.

"What's going on?" I asked, taking my usual spot at the cheerleaders' table.

"You're the first girl on our soccer team," Katie gushed.

"Ohh, yeah. I was too hungry to change out of my jersey," I said for no particular reason.

"And look at you, already rocking the jersey," Sophia complimented.

"I do look good, don't I," I agreed.

After school, I took a shower in the locker room. I dressed in a sleeveless short dress, a jacket, and my boots. I brushed my hair, grabbed my bag, and went to the parking lot. Jack was standing by his jeep.

"Wow, Andie, you look great," he praised. The comment meant a lot, coming from my best friend. He usually didn't notice what I wore.

"Thanks. I'm really sorry, Jack. I never meant to hurt you."

"I know, Andie." I saw Eli standing a few yards away. "I'll see you tomorrow, Jack," I said, going to Eli.

"Hey, Andrea. Are you ready?" he greeted.

"Yeah." I got into the passenger seat of Eli's car. "Tell me something about yourself," I requested.

"Umm... I'm an only child. Celine, Ric, and Alex are my best friends and my family. I live at the facility. I'm in my third year of med school. I'm not very interesting. I don't know what else you would want to know about me."

"What made you want to ask me out?" I asked curiously. I had never been on a date before and I didn't know what appropriate conversation was. I decided to wing it.

"You intrigue me, Andrea. I've watched me for years. We all have. I wanted to get to know you."

"Okay. What do you like to do?" I asked quickly moving on from the fact that I had been watched all my life, without my knowledge.

"I love soccer," he said, smiling widely.

"Really? I just got on the school soccer team today. Maybe you could help me out." I knew nothing about soccer. I could use all the help I could get.

"I'd be happy to," he agreed.

"Okay. I have a random question."

"Shoot."

"Is there any way to heal wolf scratches?" I asked, concerned for Jack.

"Werewolves naturally have quick healing," he informed.

"It's not for me. I scratched Jack," I admitted guiltily.

"Well. Yeah sure. There's cream at the facility that would work. Sometimes the scratches could get infected though."

"I cleaned the wounds," I informed.

"Then you don't need to worry too much. You can give him the cream tomorrow."

"Thanks."

"Have you been trying to get on the soccer team?" he asked quizzically.

"No. I was sitting on the bleachers, watching Jack and a ball flew at me. I kicked it away and it went straight into the goal. The coach gave me a jersey. I accepted it so that the jerk of a captain would keep Jack on the team."

"Is this your first date?" he asked curiously.

"Umm... people have asked me out before, and to school dances. But, I was usually too busy organizing the thing to worry about a date. I never really saw anyone I liked. I do go out with Jack though."

"Have you dated Jack?" he asked suddenly.

"No. He's my best friend and knows me better than anyone else. There's nothing more to it than that. Our relationship is perfectly platonic and I would never change anything about that. Why are you asking me about Jack?"

"You mention him in every sentence. You seem close."

"We are," I confirmed. "Like I said, he is my best friend."

After the movie, Eli was driving me home. "I'll bring you the cream later. It'll heal him in a half hour," he informed as his phone rang. "Hey, Ric... What? Yeah... I'll be there. Andrea, Celine went into labor. I have to be with her. I'll have someone else take you home," he said hurriedly.

"I don't mind staying," I promised.

He sped to the cove and got out of the car. He sprinted to the building. I followed carefully and entered the facility. I rushed to the infirmary and saw Celine writhing in pain. She was gripping Ric's hand tightly. Ric looked clueless as to what to do. Eli was brushing her hair back and Alex was rubbing her arm.

"What are you doing? Who's delivering the baby?" I demanded when I didn't see a nurse or doctor anywhere.

"It's delivering itself," Ric informed coolly.

"Idiots! Get her to a hospital," I screamed. "C'mon. Ric, move!" I ordered. I went to Eli's car and started the engine. I drove it as close to the facility as I could. They carried Celine out and I drove to the hospital. The doctors put her on a stretcher and rushed her off. We sat in the reception.

"You guys are crazy. You can't leave a woman in labor like that. The baby could have died, Ric," I chastised. A nurse came to us with a clipboard.

"Who's the next of kin for Celine Mason?" she asked brusquely. The boys looked at each other, unsure of what to do.

"Ric," I volunteered. He took the papers and signed them.

"Can I see her?" he asked.

"Not while she's in labor. Unless you're the kid's father." Ric sat back down quietly. We waited for hours. My phone rang past midnight. It was Jack's mom.

"Mrs. Russell, what's up?" I asked. It wasn't unusual for her to call me, but the hour surprised me. I hoped she and Jack were okay.

"Andrea, can you drive over?" she pleaded frantically.

"Of course. What's wrong? Where's Jack?"

"I hear groaning in his room. He's not letting me in. he sounds sick. You know he listens to you," she begged desperately.

"I'll be there soon," I promised.

"What's wrong?" Ric asked.

"Something is wrong with Jack. I have to check on him. I'll be back in a bit."

"Andrea, your scratches might have infected him. I grabbed a tin of cream from the infirmary. Here." Eli tossed a small tin to me. I caught it instinctively.

"I'm taking your car," I informed and sprinted out of the hospital. I rushed to Jack's place and knocked. Mrs. Russell let me in.

"Jack, it's Andie. Let me in," I called, knocking on the door to his room. I heard grunting and strained movement. The lock clicked open. I heard the sounds of movement again. I waited a minute before opening the door so I didn't spook him. "I'm coming in, Jack," I informed as I walked in. I saw him lying face down on his bed, under a bunch of heavy sheets.

"Shut the door, Andie. Mom, stay outside," he groaned. I looked at his mom.

"Do it dear. I just want him to be okay." I shut the door and knelt at Jack's bedside. I brushed his hair back gently. He was sweating buckets. He opened his eyes and looked at me weakly. His body was under the sheets.

"Jack, is it the scratches? Let me see. I have something that can help you." I gently lifted the sweaty sheets out of the way. He wore nothing but boxer shorts. I dropped the sheets on the floor and peeled off the bandage on his back. The wounds were still oozing blood. I braced myself before I took a dollop of cream and spread it over the cuts. He screamed into the pillow as the cream touched his open skin. Tears flowed from my eyes, hearing his screams. I used my clean hand to wipe my tears and placed it against his cheek.

"It hurts!" he shrieked.

"I know Jack. I know. One more. Just one more." I unwrapped the bandage on his arm and put some cream on it. "That's it. That's it. It'll be over soon. I'm so sorry, Jack," I sobbed. I wiped my hands on my dress and held his shuddering body tightly. I pressed my lips to his head. "Jack I'm sorry. I'll never hurt you again." I swore.

He stopped groaning fifteen minutes later. "Andie," he whispered, his voice cracking. I composed my face as he looked at me.

"Don't move for another fifteen minutes, Jack. The skin's still red," I instructed.

"Okay, Dr. Morgan," he teased. Even in his pain, he was trying to make me laugh. I wiped his tears.

"I'm sorry," I apologized again.

"Come here," he invited gently. I lay on the bed next to him, not bothering that he was dripping with sweat. He rested his head on my shoulder. "Relax, Andie. Did my mom wake you?"

"No. I was at the hospital. Celine's having her baby."

"How was your date?"

"It went well."

"You can leave, Andie. I'm feeling better already."

"I'm not leaving until your skin is back to normal."

"Where did you get that cream?"

"Eli gave it to me."

"I should probably keep it handy."

"I don't intend on hurting you again, Jack." He gave me an exasperated look. "I'll put it on your desk," I sighed.

I left an hour later and went back to the hospital. The reception was empty. I called Ric.

"Andrea, it's Alex."

"Where are you guys? I'm in the building."

"I'll come get you." I hung up and waited. Alex appeared a few minutes later.

"How's Celine?"

"She had the baby and is in a room, waiting for the nurse to bring her the baby." He led me to a room. Celine was sitting on a bed. Ric and Eli were next to her.

"Hey, Andrea," she greeted brightly.

"Hey," I said, hugging her. "How are you?"

"I'm great. Wolf healing, remember?" a nurse walked in with a bundle in her arms.

"Ms. Mason, your daughter."

"Andrea, could you bring her to me?" Celine requested.

I took the baby and carried her to Celine. "She's perfect," I complimented. I gave her to her mother.

"My precious Freya," Celine crooned, holding the baby."

"That's a beautiful name," Ric commented.

"Do you want to hold her?" Celine asked.

"Sure," Ric smiled. We watched Ric's face light up as he rocked Freya. It was 4 a.m. when we left the hospital.

"Where are you going, Andrea?" Ric asked.

"Going to walk home. I have school in a few hours."

"You're going to school? You've been up all night."

"I need the credits."

"Let me take you home."

"You should be with Celine, Ric. I'll be fine."

"Okay. Be safe."

It took me an hour to get home. I grabbed some pop tarts and showered. I dressed in shorts and my soccer jersey. It was so long it reached my thighs. I used a belt to style it like a dress and used safety pins to give it definition on my shoulders. I popped in a vervain pill and put on a moonstone anklet. I tried calling my dad. He hadn't called me since he left, which was weird. He usually called me every night he was away. I put on knee-high boots and put in a blade. I tied my hair up and decided to pamper myself with a manicure. I was going to be the most stylish soccer player in history. I watched some TV before leaving for Jack's place.

Mrs. Russell was sitting on the couch when I walked into the apartment. "Hey, is Jack okay?" I asked inquisitively.

"Yeah. Thanks again for last night," she said, her voice filled with gratitude.

"It's not a problem," I assured.

"Jack! Andie's here!" Mrs. Russell called.

"Coming," he called back.

"I heard you made the team, Andrea,"

"Yeah. It was a surprise."

Jack came out a while later. I caught him wincing slightly. I felt a twinge of guilt.

"Hey, Andie. Are you wearing your hair differently?" I touched my hair and smiled. I had styled my hair differently. It surprised me that he noticed something so trivial.

"Yeah, Jack," I drove to school and pulled into the parking lot.

"Do you think the outfit is too much?" I asked, fidgeting with the jersey.

"You could pull off a plaid bathrobe with striped socks," he teased with a hint of appreciation in his voice.

"Umm... thanks, I guess."

"How are you going to lead cheer and play soccer?" he quizzed, walking to the building.

"Cheer is after school and soccer practice is during the day."

"I just don't want to see you exhaust yourself," he said considerately.

Party poppers went off as I entered the building. "Aah!" I exclaimed. I looked around and saw the cheer squad and soccer team. There was a banner with my name on it. I was surprised by the reception I was receiving.

"Hey, guys. What's all this? Jack, did you know?" I asked, smiling.

"No," he said. "It looks like it's for you, though."

"Of course it is idiot," Katie said. Jack looked down, obviously embarrassed and a bit hurt. I put my arm around his shoulders, pulling him close to me as my anger raged. I kept my head clear and exhaled.

"Okay. That's it! If one more person takes a swing at my best friend, I'll quit cheer and soccer. As a bonus, I'll resign from the dance committee. I wonder how the homecoming dance will look," I warned, playing my trump card. I knew no one else at this school could do what I did.

"You rock, Jack," one of the soccer players said half-heartedly.

"That's more like it. Come on, Jack." I took his hand and led him past the crowd.

"Sorry, Andie. I ruined your moment," Jack apologized.

"Don't be an idiot, Jack. I owe you for the scratches. Ohh, by the way, I saw you wincing this morning. How are you?" I probed.

"I'm not sure, Andie. It hurts, but there are no scars."

"I'll ask Ric about it." I dialed Ric's number. He answered on the first ring.

"Andrea, are you alright? Is something wrong?"

"I scratched Jack yesterday, with my claws. Eli gave me some cream but Jack's still wincing."

"The claws must have gone deep. Have him put on another layer of cream and wrap it up. Be sure not to get any in your body. It's made of highly concentrated heather."

"Does that involve touching it?" I asked.

"No. The jelly makes it safe to touch, but make sure there's no open skin."

"Okay, Ric. Thanks." I hung up and turned to Jack. "You're supposed to put on some more cream and wrap it up."

"Okay. I'll do that and see you in math class."

I nodded and walked into class. Liam walked up to me.

"Hey, Morgan. I heard about your moves in cheer practice yesterday. I look forward to seeing them. Where are you headed?" he pressed.

"Umm, math class," I stated.

"I'll walk you there," he offered.

"I can manage. Thanks," I declined.

"I'm headed that way, Morgan."

"Look, Liam, just get to the point," I demanded, planting my feet and facing him.

"I like you, Morgan. I want to ask you out."

"Liam, you have to learn how to respect a woman first. My name is Andrea. How do you expect me to say yes to you, Liam? You treat my best friend like your personal punching bag. You have to work on your attitude if you ever want a girl to like you." I strode off to class and sat at my usual desk. Jack walked in a few minutes later.

"You okay?" I asked.

"Better," he assured.

I went to the locker room after class and put on my sneakers. I tied the jersey up and went out. Jack was waiting outside.

"Andie, you should put on some pads," he advised.

"I'm a werewolf, Jack," I reminded.

"No one else knows that," he said, handing me some shin guards. He helped me put them on before we went out to the field together.

Coach blew his whistle to get everyone's attention. "Gentlemen, let's all be gentle with Ms. Morgan. Teach her, don't clobber her. I'm looking at you, Liam. Ms. Morgan, try to get the ball in the goal. They'll pass you the ball.

I stood in the middle of the field. Oliver had the ball. It came flying in my direction. I ran towards it and jumped. I flipped mid-air, extending one leg, and kicked the ball. It changed direction and flew into the goal. I landed steadily on my feet and looked around.

"What was that?" coach demanded.

"Is that against the rules?" I asked, confused.

"Hell, no. Where did you learn those moves?"

"I'm a cheerleader. I do flips in mid-air every day," I shrugged.

"You hear that, boys? Cheerleading is not mandatory for you idiots."

"What?" we all asked.

"I've never seen any of you boys do that. You are going to learn that in cheer practice. Ms. Morgan, you're going to teach them."

"Coach, cheerleading is really hard. You need to know quite a bit of gymnastics to try it. It takes years to learn how to do what I just did," I protested.

"You're going to try. Now, go again."

I spent an hour on the field until I laid flat on the field.

"I'm done," I announced.

"Okay. Boys, remember to meet her for cheer practice at..."

"The gym after school," I finished. "Wear something you can move in."

Liam came up to me. "Can I help you?" he asked.

"I'm fine, thanks."

"You have great moves, Andrea."

I nodded as Jack pulled me up. I threw his arm around his shoulder.

"That was great, Andrea. Was that wolf stuff or cheerleading?"

"Mostly cheer, but it feels like everything is slowing down, which helps me get every move down perfectly."

"Do you think I could do that?" he asked eagerly.

"I think you can do anything you set your mind to. You should know, cheerleading is one of the hardest things I've done. But, I'd love to teach you."

"Okay. Not your best pep talk," he teased.

"I'll personally make sure you don't break anything," I promised.

"Are you talking about the floor or bleachers?"

"Your back or limbs," I corrected. He gulped nervously and I punched his shoulder lightly.

"Well, if I'm going to be flying through the air, I'm glad one of us has werewolf reflexes." After the last period, I turned to Jack.

"Hey, I have to go change. I'll meet you at the gym in a few minutes." I went to the locker room and changed into my cheer uniform. I ponytailed my hair and went to the gym.

"Hey, ladies," I said. "As you can see, we have some guests. The soccer players will be joining us. Let's get started. Guys get down here. Okay...split up into pairs or groups of three with a cheerleader guys."

Jack and Liam both approached me.

"Will you be my teacher?" Liam asked.

"No, I'm with Jack... Okay. Today we're going to do some basic gymnastics moves. Let's start with handstands."

"I have never done one of those in my life," Jack commented.

"I'll show you. Ladies, positions." We all stood up straight and kicked up into a handstand. We then let our legs drop into a bridge and stood back up. "Jack, come on. Back straight, arms up, parallel to each other. Put one leg in front of the other. Now, bend forward. Don't worry there are mats to cushion your fall. Kick your legs up." I positioned my arms to catch him. "Keep pressure in your stomach." He kicked his legs but fell on his back before I could catch him.

"Owww," he groaned. I pulled him to his feet.

"Try again, Jack. This time, I'll hold you up." He stood up and bent forward. I bent over him, reaching for his legs. I used my werewolf muscles to pull them up.

"Woah!" he exclaimed.

"Easy, Jack, It's just me. Keep your arms steady... I'm going to let go of your legs." I did and moved one arm behind his legs. "Guys!" I called, noticing that no one was having much luck. "Why don't we try against the wall and just get this down today?" I suggested. There were murmurs of assent all around me. I led Jack to a wall and gestured for him to go for it.

"How am I supposed to do this, Andie?" he asked, baffled.

"Just kick, Jack. I'll help you," I promised. He bent over and kicked with all his strength until his legs touched the wall. I put my hands in front of his legs, barely touching them but ready to catch him if necessary. "That's great, hold it," I encouraged. I helped him drop his legs a few seconds later. We spent the rest of the hour doing handstands.

"Is cheer really this hard?" Jack asked genuinely.

"Harder, dude," I informed with a grimace.

"You make it look easy," he appreciated.

"I've had years of practice Jack. You'll get it." I grabbed my stuff and went to the parking lot. I was on the way to my car when Eli approached me.

"Hey," he greeted. I smiled at him. "I saw you on the field today. You're a natural," he praised.

"Thanks," I grinned.

"Are you coming to the facility now?"

"Yeah. I just have to find Jack," I said absentmindedly, searching for Jack. Liam walked up to me.

"Hey Andrea," he said, trying to put his arm over my shoulders.

"Who's he?" Eli asked defensively.

"I'm her boyfriend," Liam announced.

"What?" Eli asked possessively before I could react. He turned away from us and strode off in the opposite direction.

"What's wrong with you, Liam," I reprimanded, shoving him away. I got in my car and Jack got in a few moments later.

"Hey, Andie,"

"I'm going to the facility. Do you want to come?" I asked, not bothering to exchange pleasantries.

"Sure, no problem." I drove to the cove and we went inside. I immediately went to find Eli. I asked for directions to his room and knocked before I walked inside.

"Hey," I said in an apologetic tone.

"Hi," he replied dejectedly.

"Eli," I began, sitting next to him. I gently put my palm on his shoulder. "Liam's a jerk. I let him take me to a dance for Jack's sake. Liam said he'd let Jack onto the soccer team if I went with him. Nothing else happened," I explained, making my voice as trustworthy as I could.

Eli turned to look at me and rested his head on my collarbone. At that moment, I knew how much he really liked me. We weren't officially together yet, but he was still possessive over me. I rubbed his back for a few moments. The door opened again and Alex paced in.

"Hey, Andrea. I heard you were here. Come see Celine," he invited. I looked at Eli who had looked up as Alex entered the room. He met my eyes for a second, measuring them. "Unless you two are busy," Alex tacked on.

"No," Eli said, standing up. He extended his arm in my direction, an offer and an acceptance. "Come on, Andrea." I stood and took his hand, his fingers intertwined with mine.

"Where's Ric?" I asked Alex.

"He's with Celine,"

"Are they back together?" I asked eagerly.

"Not officially," he replied with a smile. We went to Celine's room. There was a crib next to her bed, it was empty at the moment. Celine was holding her daughter. Celine and Ric looked at us as we entered and smiled in greeting. I perched gently on the bed, next to Celine.

"Hi Freya," I cooed.

There was an urgent knock on the door a while later. I opened it. "Miss Andrea, it's you friend," a boy said, obviously winded from running to get me.

"Jack? What happened?" I demanded frantically.

"The training mats," was all the boy managed to get out before I pushed him out of the way. I sprinted downstairs, to the training area. I skidded to a stop in front of Jack's motionless form on the mat.

"Jack!" I exclaimed, collapsing next to him. I pulled his head onto my lap, my breathing uneven. I shouldn't have left him alone here. I should have made sure he stayed by my side. "What happened to him?" I choked.

"He was on the floor when we got here?" someone answered.

"Sprinkle some water on him," Ric instructed. Someone brought me a glass of water. My fingers trembled as I used them to sprinkle water on Jack's face. Ric knelt next to me.

"Jack, look at me?" I pleaded, tears pooling in my eyes. He opened his eyes moments later.

"Andie," he groaned, trying to focus on me.

"Jack!" I exclaimed through my tears. I brushed his hair back. "What happened? Do you hurt anywhere?"

"I'm fine Andie. I was trying to do that move you showed us at cheer practice," he admitted.

"On your own?" I demanded, furious now.

"Andrea," Ric intervened. "You can question him later. Let's get him up." Ric helped him to his feet and I threw my arms around him.

"I should get you home. Ric, I'll see you tomorrow," I led Jack to my car and helped him safely in. "What were you thinking Jack? Why were you trying to do that on your own?" I asked as gently as I could. I was terrified at the thought of how badly my best friend might have been hurt.

"You've been pulling my weight, Andie. I just wanted to show you that I could do it," he admitted, looking down.

"Jack. I'm not Liam or the coach or Katie. You don't have to prove anything to me," I assured.

9

I walked onto the soccer field two days later.

"We were waiting for you," the coach informed me stiffly. The rest of the team was huddled around him.

"What's going on?" I asked.

"You know there's a dance tonight, right?"

That was obvious. "Of course I do. I organized it," I stated. "It's for the first game of the season, tomorrow."

"Exactly. Attendance is mandatory for all of you. I'm going to show you off. Be ready and come prepared."

"What you mean, ready?" I asked warily.

"For you, Ms. Morgan, it includes a dress and a date."

"Where do I find a date?" I asked, throwing my hands up in exasperation.

"Just grab a friend," he said as if it was the most obvious thing in the world.

"Jack?" I asked hoping he would come to my rescue, looking at him. He smiled and nodded. So did the coach.

"For the rest of you, it means clothes that aren't covered in sweat and dirt," he instructed.

Jack dropped me off later that afternoon.

"I'll come back in a while to pick you up," he promised.

I went into my apartment to find Ric on the couch.

"What are you doing here?" I asked.

"I just thought I'd see if you were coming home or to the facility," he answered coolly.

"Ohh. That was nice of you. There's a game tomorrow night. Will you come? I'll be playing."

"Sure, I'd love to see you play."

"Great. I have to get ready," I said, excusing myself.

"What? Didn't you say the game was tomorrow?"

"It is. There's a dance this evening. Jack will be here soon." I went into my room and showered. I dressed in a dark blue, thigh-length dress. It was completely fitted and had a lacy back and short sleeves. I brushed my hair down and put on black boots. I stuck a blade in it and put on a moonstone bracelet. I put on some makeup and went back to the couch.

"You look like you were raised by werewolves. Beautiful," Ric complimented graciously.

"Thanks,"

"Do you have any plans this weekend?" he asked suddenly.

"Not really. Why?"

"I thought we could fit in some more training."

"Sure. I'll be at the facility," I agreed.

Jack knocked on the door and I answered it. Jack was holding a beautiful red rose. He knew exactly what I liked.

"Thanks, Jack. I'll go get some water." I filled a transparent glass with water and set it on my dresser, I put the rose in and went back to the door with my phone.

"Are you ready?"

"Yeah. See you, Ric...Jack, it's not prom," I teased gently. He was holding the door of his jeep open for me. "But thanks." The gesture was sweet. I got in careful not to crumple my dress and he drove to school.

"Do you think I should have worn my jersey?" Jack asked awkwardly. He was wearing a plain T-shirt and jeans.

"You look great," I reassured. The gym was already packed when we walked in. Confetti fell around us as we crossed the threshold.

"Now that everyone's finally here," the coach began with a pointed glare toward Jack and me. "Give it up for this year's soccer team," he announced. "Captain Liam and Vice-Captain Oliver... our newest member, Jackson Russell, and your cheer captain, Andrea Morgan." I waved confidently at everyone. I knew everyone at school loved me. "I know you're all wondering what a girl is doing on our soccer team. You should come check her out tomorrow."

The music started again. "Dance with me, Andie," Jack invited.

"I'm not a great dancer," I protested quietly. In reality, I loved to dance, but I preferred not to in public.

"Humor me." I smiled and let him lead me out. We danced for a while and then sat at a table. "Are you having fun?"

"It's great, Jack, really." Liam and Oliver joined us with a plate of appetizers.

"Do you want to dance?" Liam asked me.

"Sure. Come on, Jack," I scoffed, turning away from Liam. There was one person I could avoid dancing with. This time, I pulled him out as a slow song started. I reached up and placed my arms around his neck. He put his palms on my waist and spun me around in time with the music.

Jack drove me home hours later. I walked into my apartment. "Ric? I thought you would have gone back to the institute," I said.

"I thought I'd stay here tonight. If that's okay."

"Yeah. Sure. Make yourself comfortable. Is there anything you wanted to talk about?"

"I just wanted to be around. You've been alone here. I just wanted to be your brother."

"Thanks," I said with emotion.

"How was the dance?"

"It was fun. I'm sorry. I'm so exhausted, I'm going to bed." I really was tired. I felt like I might fall asleep standing up.

The next evening I was in the locker room. I used a rubber band to pull my jersey aside and ponytailed my hair. I took my sneakers and padded out to the field. Jack met me on the bench and double-knotted my laces for me.

"Are you ready?" I asked.

"What?"

"It's your first game," I explained.

"Yeah. I'm all set," he said reassuringly.

I went to the cheerleaders. "I'll be cheering on the field guys. Try to mimic my moves. Make me proud." Most of my soccer technique was based on cheerleading. I was sure the cheerleaders would be able to pull out the moves I was performing. I went to the huddle in the middle of the field.

"Andrea, you're on offense. Jack, you are on defense. The rest of you know what you're supposed to do. All of you cover Andrea. She can score, but she's not great at taking the ball or protecting it yet. Oliver, I want you on her position. Liam keep your eye on her but don't shadow her. You have to lead the boys. Make sure you all pass her the ball. If you don't think she can receive the pass, aim for Oliver who will pass to Andrea. Watch each other's backs," the coach ordered.

"Where do I stand?" I asked.

"Liam will show you." I reluctantly let Liam lead me out. He positioned me where he wanted me and signaled Oliver over. Oliver stood a few feet away from me, his eyes trained on me. I saw Ric, Eli, and Alex in the stands. A few minutes into the game, the ball came flying to me. I jumped into a backflip and extended one of my legs. I kicked the ball with it and landed steadily. The ball flew into the goal. I saw the cheerleaders doing synchronized backflips. The next time, I did a cartwheel, my leg hitting the ball in the air. I scored every time I got the ball. Right before half-time, I launched myself into the air. I flipped twice and kicked the ball. It was a move I had done a million times in the gym. I was confident that I would stick the landing. My foot slipped as it touched the ground. I probably landed on a slippery patch of grass. I landed on my back, but luckily the ball flew true as the whistle rang.

"Urgh," I groaned. The coach and Liam were the first to reach me. My vision was a little blurry. I wondered how badly I was injured.

"Andrea, are you okay?" the coach demanded frantically. "Come on. Try to stand up. Liam help her." Liam pulled my arm over his shoulder and wound his arm around my waist. He helped me to my feet. I didn't like being pressed against him. I could barely stand but I was very uncomfortable leaning on Liam.

"Jack," I breathed, pushing Liam away weakly.

"Damn Andie. I'm here," he said breathlessly. I could tell he had run across the field for me. He took Liam's place, pushing him away with more force, and supported my weight. "Andie, can you hear me?"

"I'm fine," I lied unconvincingly.

"Shut up. You're not okay," he chastised. My trembling legs gave way and Jack hurried to lift me up into his arms. He groaned quietly as he bore all my weight in his arms.

"Does she have family here?" the coach asked Jack. "She fell hard. She could have broken something."

"Her brother, Ric," Jack gasped. I could tell he couldn't bear my weight.

"Jack, set me down," I demanded, my voice no louder than a whisper. Coach used his megaphone to signal Ric. Ric sprinted over and skidded to a stop in front of us.

"Give her to me, Jack. I'll take her," Ric said. I was grateful for that offer. Jack's breaths were labored and I knew Ric could carry me easily.

"Andrea, it's Ric," he informed unnecessarily.

"Ric," I acknowledged.

"You're okay. I'm here," he promised.

"Andrea, you're on the bench for the rest of the night," the coach decided.

"No coach, I have to play," I protested weakly. I have to admit, I probably didn't look very stable, lying limp in Ric's arms.

"You'll get me arrested. I should be shipping you to a hospital, but I'll leave that decision to your brother," the coach stated blandly. Ric carried me to the bench and Jack followed. Eli and Alex were waiting to help Ric set me down. I slumped against Eli's side as he gave me a bottle of water.

"That fall would have broken anyone else's back, Andrea. You'll probably heal by morning," Ric whispered.

"It hurts," I moaned into Eli's shoulder.

"That's proof that it's healing," Eli murmured, putting his arm around me.

"I've done that move a million times," I complained.

"No one's perfect. You're staying at the facility tonight, where we can keep an eye on you," Ric ordered. I didn't protest. Jack came up to us after the game.

"Are you going home?" I asked.

"Umm... victory pizza actually. I wish you could join us." I was happy that the other players invited Jack along.

"Next time, Jack," I promised. "Have fun."

"What about you?"

"I'm going to the facility. I'll be fine."

After Jack left, Ric stood up. He picked me up. "I can walk," I protested. He glared at me, refusing to set me down.

"Come on, Andrea," he said authoritatively. He carried me to the backseat of his car and helped me in. He carried me into the facility.

"When can I walk?" I asked as he set me lightly on my feet. He let go of me and as if by design, Eli took his place.

"When you've had rest. Eli, take her to her room. I have to see Celine. I'll drop in on you in a bit."

Eli carried me up. Every movement caused me pain. I tried to hide it. As soon as Eli set me down, I laid face forward on my bed.

"Andrea, can I bring you dinner?" Eli asked, lightly touching my shoulder.

"I'm not really hungry."

"Tea, or some coffee?" he pressed.

"A cup of tea sounds nice," I accepted.

"I'll be right back with that." I shrugged into my pajamas. Ric came in a while later.

"I have your tea. I sent Eli to bed." He helped me sit up and I had some tea. Then, he gave me an ice pack. I laid back down and he put it on my back.

"Ohh. That feels great," I sighed.

"I'll be right here, attending to your needs," he promised as he kissed my head gently.

"Thanks, Ric."

"Any time, Andrea. Sweet dreams."

10

I woke up in the morning and stretched, braced for the pain. I was surprised to find my back completely healed. I dressed in jeans and a T-shirt. I stuck a sword in my belt and went to Celine's room.

"How are you feeling?" she asked.

"All healed. Where's my brother?"

"Umm," she hesitated, debating whether to tell me or not. "There was some disturbance in the city. He's in the main hall." I went downstairs and found a big crowd.

"What's going on?" I demanded, standing next to Ric.

"There have been Dokkalfar in the city for weeks now," Ric lamented.

"What? Didn't you check that out last week?" I asked.

"The case just went to the FBI. The icy homicides all over the city are theirs. The body count is over five thousand. I should have noticed earlier." I could hear the stress in his voice.

"What do they want?"

"This is how it started last time. They're letting us know they're here."

"What do we do?"

"You aren't doing anything," he said quickly. "We have to find them."

"Ric, I've been training," I protested.

"I can't let anything happen to you. You're not ready."

"Ric, she's Lilian's daughter. She won't take no for an answer. I'll take care of her. I assure her safety," Eli said. I gave him a thankful smile and then smirked at Ric.

"It's settled. What do I do?"

Ric shook his head. "Get yourself an energy bar and come to the war council."

"What?"

"The conference room is where we talk about war policies. Eli will bring you there." He left hurriedly and I went to the breakfast table. I grabbed an energy bar and washed it down with a glass of apple juice. Eli led me to a room with guards and wolves in front. It seemed well protected. We went in and I saw Ric at the head of the table. Alex was on his left and Eli sat next to Alex. Celine was on the second seat to Ric's right.

"Andrea, this is your seat," he informed. I took the seat on his immediate right and looked around. There were pack elders and people who looked like soldiers. "You all know Andrea, my sister. She will be a part of this discussion. Andrea, we have Andrew and Lise here. They are FBI agents."

"We asked to be put on the case, hoping it would help us find the Dokkalfar before the humans did," Andrew said.

"And what did you find?" I wasn't sure my questions would be answered immediately.

"Just bodies, mam," he answered. His tone and respect took me off guard.

"Please, call me Andrea," I might be some kind of royalty here, but I was only seventeen years old. I didn't think it was right for people so much older than me to address me that way.

"Just bodies, Andrea," he amended. "They want us to find them."

"Then we'll find them. Take them down," I offered eagerly.

"Hold on," Ric intervened authoritatively. "Andrea, hold on a moment. I want surveillance all around the city. All entrances to New York have to be watched. Double troops after sunset. I want updates every hour, on the hour. I'll personally check on all the troops after dusk. Have enough matches, torches, and flashlights. Stock your weapons carefully. Lise, I need you behind the desk on this one. Be our ears. Andrew, you can lead a troop. Try to catch one. I want to know what they are planning. Dismissed," Ric commanded.

Ric was looking at a file of photographs. "These are the victims," he said, sliding them over to me after everyone else left the room. The bodies looked frostbitten and covered in powdered ice. All the victims had identical masks of horror.

"They look terrified," I stated blatantly.

"Andrea, the ones in our facility were never trained. Dokkalfar are fierce and deadly. Their very breath could kill you. They have heavy, black war regalia. You have to be faster than lightning to take one down. If you kill one, it'll start a war between our people. That could disrupt our city's peace. We have to be careful and discreet."

"What do I do then? I can't sit here doing nothing!" I exclaimed.

"You're going to learn how to shoot today," he informed me, as coolly as if he was reading off of a schedule. "Archery and guns. If you're going to fight, you need to know this."

"What will you be doing?"

"Monitoring the city. Getting the facility ready for battle. Celine is in the training area. I'll find you if there's anything new."

I went to Celine. She was ready to spring into action. "Come on, Andrea. Try this bow. How does it feel?"

"How is it supposed to feel?" I asked, confused. I had never touched a bow before.

"Is it balanced or heavy or light?" she explained.

"Balanced, I guess." I couldn't really tell. I'd never tried archery before.

"Good. Shoulder your quiver and draw an arrow." I slung the sheath of arrows over my shoulder and reached back to pull out an arrow. She helped me notch the arrow and aim. It took me all morning to learn how to aim. Then we switched to guns. They were easier than the bow and arrow.

"How's she doing?" Ric asked when he came to check on me that evening.

"She's brilliant. She's a natural. Look at the target. With a little practice, she could be better than me.

"Fantastic, Andrea. I'm going on patrol. Do you want to come?"

"Sure," my arms ached from shooting all day but I wasn't going to miss an opportunity to be useful.

"Get some weapons and we can go." I tucked knives into my boots and put my sword in my belt. Celine helped me put a gun in a holster on my thigh. She procured a trench coat.

"Use this, Andrea. It's cold out and this will hide your weapons better." I pulled it on, being careful not to rip it. "Can you walk comfortably?"

"Yeah," I replied and went to Ric.

"We'll be walking all around the city. Are you up for it?" I nodded. He led me to a sleek mountain jeep – as if a jeep could be called sleek – and got in. I carefully climbed into my seat and put my seatbelt on. We spent all night checking on the troops strategically positioned around the city. Just before dawn, we were at Brooklyn Bridge. A man walked up to us purposefully.

"We have one that wants to negotiate," he told Ric.

"Set up a meeting at the cove in two hours, to talk."

"Why do we have to wait?" I asked curiously.

"I need to get to Alex. Make sure the meeting place is dark enough. I don't want to kill them before I know what they have to offer," he told the man, simultaneously answering my question.

"Of course," the man replied immediately. Ric and I got into the jeep and rushed to the facility.

"Why does it have to be dark?" I asked.

"Dokkalfar are sensitive to sunlight. I want them to tell me everything."

"I'm coming with you," I stated.

"Andrea," he began.

"Ric, I'm your sister. And, if what you all claim is true, I'm going to be the alpha someday," I protested.

I got out of the jeep and went up to my room in the facility. I dressed in a tank top and fresh jeans. I brushed my hair and replaced my moonstones. I rushed back to the war council.

"We were waiting for you," Ric informed. "I chose our territory because we know how to defend and protect it. We'll be meeting in a dark clearing. Celine, Alex, and Eli, you're with me. Andrea, you can come. Alex, Eli, she's your responsibility. Celine, I want your best shooters all around the clearing, providing us with cover. Even if they ask us to come in unarmed, I want a concealed weapon on all of you. Orion will come with us. He will be Andrea's last line of defense. Celine, tell your soldiers to take their wolves. Hope will be stationed outside Freya's room. I want guards at every entrance to the facility. A troop will be in the basement. Elders, please stay inside. Remember, Andrea is the rightful alpha. If things go sideways, she is the first priority. Get her to safety."

"Ric," Celine interrupted. "If the elders are going to be inside, maybe they could stay with Freya."

"Sure. When we are out there, I want everyone to be alert. Be ready for anything. Now, go get breakfast."

"What about you?" I asked Ric as he stayed in his seat while everyone filed out.

"I'm not hungry."

"Stop, Ric, come on."

"Miss Andrea, there's someone here for you," a lady said. I went out to see Jack. I hugged him gently.

"Andie, are you okay?"

"I'm great, Jack."

"I mean your back."

"It healed yesterday morning, Jack."

"What have you been doing? You didn't call me or text."

"I'm sorry, Jack. It's a warzone here. The elves are in our city. I've been on patrols with Ric all night. We have a negotiation in a little while."

"What can I do?" he asked eagerly.

"Stay alive," Ric intervened. "Go upstairs. You'll see a room with guards. There are kids there. Stay there. Take a gun. You can shoot right?"

"Yeah. In theory," he replied uncertainly.

"Get a gun from Celine and go up. You can help guard or you can wait inside."

"Okay. Andie, be careful. I don't like the idea of you out there."

"Neither do I, but she'll be safe," Ric promised.

Jack hugged me again, shot a glance at Ric, and left. Ric and I had a hurried breakfast and I went to stock up on weapons. Someone had sharpened my sword for me. I put it in my belt and put two blades on my arms. I slipped one into my boots. Celine had a full quiver and a scary-looking bow. She had two guns strapped to her legs. Alex was wearing a vest filled with blades, a shield, and a sword. Eli had a sword in his belt and a double-ended spear. Ric had two twin swords and a gun in his belt.

"Andrea, stay close. Orion!" Ric called. Orion came bounding over and stood in front of me. I followed Ric through the cove. I saw soldiers and wolves all around the woods. "Remember, no sudden movements." Ric entered the clearing first. Celine and Orion followed him. I followed, between Alex and Eli. Alex made me feel safe.

I looked at the Dokkalfar and felt a shiver run down my spine. They had white skin that was stretched over their sharp bones. They had pointy noses and their red eyes shone brightly under their obsidian helmets. They had heavy black robes to shield themselves from the light. The elves behind the leader had medieval weapons; axes, clubs, morning stars, and basic swords.

"I am commander of the king," the elf said.

"Brother of the Alpha of the Eclipse pack of Brooklyn," Ric announced. He was obviously presenting himself as a commander. He didn't draw attention to the fact that I was the alpha but made it clear that he wasn't the leader.

"Let us put down the weapons away and talk,"

Ric nodded and we all took off our weapons. I left a blade in each of my legs.

"What do you have for us?" Ric commanded.

"You are familiar with the agent Nicolas Morgan?" the elf asked monotonously. That was my dad's name. I focused harder.

"Yes," Ric answered, revealing nothing.

"We have him with us. You have our princes. We want them in return for the agent," they demanded.

"Lilian Velvela. We want her body too," Ric countered.

"What do you want with a dead body?"

"We owe her a funeral. She should rest with her ancestors. Do you have her or not?"

"Our people reveled in taking an alpha. We have her," he confirmed.

"Lilian and the agent for your princes," Ric stated.

"Done. We make the trade tomorrow night at Brooklyn Bridge."

The elves turned and marched away. I turned to Ric, words failing me. I couldn't believe that my dad was taken by the same creatures that killed my mom. He was just an officer. My mother was a trained killing machine and she couldn't survive the Dokkalfar. I was terrified for my father.

"Shh," Ric cautioned. I felt faint and leaned back. Alex caught me before I hit the ground and held me up against him. I was about to sob and he covered my mouth with his hand. I let him support me since I didn't trust my legs to hold me up. Eli tried to comfort me.

"They're gone. Let her go," Ric assured. Alex did and I was falling forward. Ric grabbed me and held me tight. I still couldn't talk. I struggled to clear my throat.

"They have dad," I cried.

"We'll get your dad back, Andrea. I swear," he assured.

"I can't breathe," I choked. He picked me up and carried me into the building. My head bobbed against Ric's chest as he walked. "Ric," I sighed.

"I'm here. Right here," he promised. He sat me on a couch in one of the lounges off the main hall. "Look at me. Your dad's okay. They'll let him go tomorrow night Andrea." A man came over to us.

"Is it done?" he asked. I almost recognized the voice.

"Yeah, Ollie," he replied, not looking at him. I looked up to see the soccer player, Oliver.

"What? Who's this?" I demanded in shock. Jack came down and stopped in his tracks.

"Andie, what's he doing here?" Jack demanded.

"Ric?" I asked.

"Andrea, this is Lilian's foster son. A born werewolf. Our foster brother," Ric introduced.

"Does he know who I am?" I demanded.

"I do. Hi, Andrea," Oliver smiled.

"How could you have been so awful to me when you knew that we were family?" I asked, too exhausted to hide my hurt.

"I had to keep my cover, Andrea."

"And Jack?" I asked, through my tears.

"It was so that I could stay around Liam," I didn't understand that logic but I couldn't think straight.

"Does he know?"

"No. Jack, I never had anything against you. Andrea, I've loved you for as long as I know you existed," he confessed.

"I can't deal with this now. Jack!" I called.

"Hey Andie, what's wrong?" he asked, approaching me.

"They took my dad," I breathed in between sobs.

"Ohh my god, Andie, I'm so sorry," Jack lamented. He hugged me and I buried my face in his shoulder. I let him comfort me.

"Andrea, I want you to go home tonight. Jack and Ollie will be with you in school tomorrow and then come straight here," Ric instructed.

"I can't leave," I protested.

"You're not in any condition to help out here. Please, go home. I'll come check on you later."

"Does Oliver have to come?"

"He's a trained warrior and can protect you. Trust me, he loves you. You may not believe it, but believe me. I wanted to wait for the perfect time to introduce you." I nodded desolately and followed Jack to his jeep. Eli followed with my weapons and Oliver trailed behind. Jack got in the driver's seat and I climbed in the back. Oliver got in with me.

"Come here," he invited gently.

"No, thanks,"

"Andrea, please, let me in."

"Look, you may be my brother or something but you're a bully."

"Andie, it's okay. If he's your brother, it excuses his bad behavior. I forgive it. Oliver, go ahead, she won't kick you," Jack assured. I decided not to argue with Jack. Oliver assumed my silence to be acceptance. Oliver moved closer to me and put his arm around me. I was exhausted and terrified for my dad. At home, I went to my room and shut the door. I leaned on the wall and slid to the floor. I cried and could hear my sobs echoing around the room. The door opened and I was vaguely aware of two people walking in. Jack knelt in front of me and pulled my head onto his shoulder.

"I'm sure Ric will get your dad back," he assured. I cried myself to sleep, in Jack's arms.

11

I woke with a start. "Jack! Ric!" I screamed. I had had a terrible nightmare. Oliver burst through the door.

"Hey, hey. It's okay. You're safe," he said. It was too fast to be soothing.

"Where's Jack?" I demanded.

"Home. It's 5:30 a.m."

"What are you doing here?"

"Ric wanted me here to protect you."

"Okay. I'm going to go for a run," I said for no apparent reason.

"Since when do you run?"

"Today. I'm going to Central Park."

"I'll drive you."

"I'll be fine." No matter what Jack said, I wasn't ready to trust him completely yet.

"I'm not letting you go alone. I'd like to talk to you."

"About what, Oliver?" I asked, finally facing him, exasperated.

"Us."

"Talk," I accepted grudgingly. I was pretty sure he wouldn't let me get away without talking to him.

"I honestly have loved you for years, Andrea. I acted mean so I could stay with Liam. He's been obsessed with you for the longest time, so he notices things about you that I don't. I figured it would be useful to have him around."

"Do you want a trophy? You're not my blood."

"Mom thought I was her blood," he said silently.

"Well, mom's not here and all I want to do is talk to my dad about all this and he's gone too," I said, my voice cracking. Oliver wrapped his arms around me gently. I let him hug me.

"Why don't we go on a wolf run? I've always felt like it helped me release some steam. We can check on the troops and then you can get ready for school," he suggested.

"Okay." I went into the bathroom and stripped down. I let the wolf out and was on all fours. Oliver was in his wolf form, waiting for me. We ran around the city until we ran into Celine.

"Andrea, Ollie, what are you doing?" she asked.

"Just a run," I thought at her.

"Oliver, you should get to the facility and get ready for school. I'll take Andrea home. Tell Ric that I'll be back after she leaves."

"Okay. I'll keep an eye on her at school," he thought. I got into Celine's car while I was still a wolf. I turned back to my human form in my bathroom. I showered and dressed in a sports bra, a half-buttoned shirt, and shorts. I ponytailed my hair and put a blade in each of my boots. I put my phone in my pocket and went to the living room.

"Andrea, you should have some breakfast."

"I can't think about that right now. I just have to get through the day."

"You need your energy," she pressed. I tried to stay calm. "Your eyes, Andrea."

"What?"

"They're glowing," she informed me. I shut my eyes and focused on my breathing. "Andrea, do you need anything?"

"No. I just need to go. Stay active."

"Maybe I should come with you. I can be invisible in school."

"No thanks. I'll be with Jack." I took a tin of the heather gel. Celine put a bottle of apple juice in my bag.

"You have to call us if you need help." I went to my car and drove to Jack's.

"Hey, Andie. Maybe I should drive."

"I'm fine. I got it."

"Your claws are hurting the steering wheel." I exhaled and inhaled deeply. I touched my moonstone necklace, hoping it would help.

"Jack, can you get my jewelry from my bag? Maybe wearing more would help me stay in control." I put on a bracelet and ring. My claws retracted. I drove to the school and parked. "Jack, stay with me. I need help."

"I'm not going anywhere," he promised. The door of my car opened.

"Andrea," Oliver said.

"I'm fine," I protested. "Jack's with me. Excuse me, I'll be in the gym."

"What about bio?" Jack asked.

"Skipping it." I didn't have enough patience to sit in class.

"I'll come watch you," he replied instantly.

I went to the gym and took off my shirt. I took a few deep breaths and started stretching before training. When I was done, I started jumping and flipping. Oliver came in silently. "Andrea, you could get some training in. Come on."

"Who do I train with?" I demanded breathlessly.

"Me, of course."

"I've been practicing," I warned him.

"I know. Let's see how you do against me. Celine may be our best shooter, but I've heard that I'm the best at blade combat that the elders have seen."

"Don't go easy on me," I instructed.

He attacked first and I let my rage out. I punched and dodged. He caught my arms. I jumped and twisted in mid-air, landing on his shoulders. I tightened my legs around him and was about to use my upper body weight to push him to the ground. He reached up, putting one hand on my back and the other on my stomach, pulling me off his shoulders. He flipped and landed on his feet.

"Again, Andrea," I tossed my head back and punched him. I jumped, tucking my body as I flipped, landing behind him. I pushed him to the mat, face down, and straddled him. I pinned his arms behind his back.

"Okay. Okay, Andrea, let me go," he requested.

I got off his back and he stood up. "Remember, I said blade combat, not hand-to-hand," he reminded, trying to salvage his pride.

"I don't have my sword, it's in my car," was all I could say in return.

"I'll go get it for you. Remember, you have blades strapped to your legs that you can use." He came back and threw me my sword. He had a long blade. He was right, he was amazing with it. He had the blade at my throat in seconds. We kept going for the rest of the hour.

"I'm going to put the sword away and get ready for cheer practice." I pulled on my shirt and went to the locker room. I changed into my uniform and went back to the gym. The cheerleaders and soccer team were waiting.

"Today, we're going to turn our handstands into backbends. Girls, let's show them."

We stood straight and bent forward. We kicked up and held our handstands for a second before letting our legs drop gently. We used our hands to push ourselves to our feet.

"Today, I need half of you on cheer and the others with the soccer team." I turned to Jack. "I don't want you to try this without me, Jack, please."

"Okay." I helped him up into a handstand. "Hold it, Jack... good." I put one arm behind his back and used the other to support his legs. "Jack, I've got you. Do you trust me?"

"You know I do," he confirmed confidently.

"Okay. Lean your legs on my arm. Keep them loose."

"Andie, don't let me fall," he pleaded. I felt the weight of his legs against my arms. I slowly moved the arm supporting his legs, while keeping the other one steady. His legs dropped slowly and touched the mat.

"Jack, that's great. I'm going to let go. Hold it for a few seconds." I let go of his legs and then bent over, holding his back while holding one hand behind his arms. "Push yourself up, Jack. I'll help you." I helped him pull himself to his feet.

"Did I do it?" he asked.

"Jack, that was great." I noticed the entire room watching us.

"How did you do that, Russell?" Liam demanded.

"I trust her," Jack replied simply.

"I think that's the key to this," I intervened before things could get too heated. "When we were taught, we had to trust our instructor. Guys, you have to trust that we'll support you."

"What's next, Andie," Jack asked eagerly.

"Well, first you have to do this without my support," I teased.

After cheer practice, I traded my uniform for my jersey. Jack was waiting outside the locker room.

"How do you feel?" he asked considerately.

"I want to keep active," I replied curtly. We walked onto the field.

"Andrea that was great work you did on Friday. Today, boys, I want to challenge her. There'll be multiple soccer balls on the field, you will pass to her and she'll try to score. Are you ready, Andrea?"

"Yeah, I'm up for a challenge." I stood in the middle of the field. I felt claws press into my palms and fangs against my lips. I hoped being active would put them away. I launched myself into the air, clearing my mind of all emotion. A half-hour later, a feral snarl ripped through my teeth instinctively as I missed a goal.

"Try again, Ms. Morgan," the coach called. I felt the wolf trying to break free.

"Excuse me," I said, running off. I stripped down in the locker room. I let the wolf out and growled. Someone came in and I slashed blindly with my claws.

"Easy, Andie," I heard Jack caution. I realized I attacked Jack. That was enough to bring me to my senses. I went behind the lockers and turned human. I dressed hurriedly and ran to Jack.

"Are you okay? I'm so sorry, Jack," I gushed.

"You didn't get me," he reassured.

"I have blood on my fingers," I protested as I focused behind Jack. I saw Oliver's shirt in tatters. I covered my mouth with my blood stained hand. "Oliver, I'm so sorry. I didn't mean to,"

"It's okay, Andrea. I'll heal soon."

"Are you sure?" I pressed.

"Yeah. You and Jack should get back out. I'll change my shirt and see you there."

I nodded and Jack and I went back out.

"Sorry, coach," I apologized.

"Get back out there," was all he said in return. Jack and I went to the cafeteria for lunch, after practice. I sat in my usual spot at the cheerleaders‘ table.

"Behind you, Andie," Katie stage-whispered a while later.

"What?" I asked.

"Oliver's behind you," she replied, giving me a sly smile. I whipped my head around.

"Hey, ladies," he said loudly, before bending to whisper in my ear, "Andrea, we have to go." I nodded discreetly and he left. I followed inconspicuously a few minutes later. I went to the locker room and put on my shirt. I went to my car and he got in the passenger seat.

"What's wrong?" I demanded immediately.

"Ric's starting preparations for tonight. He thought you'd like to be there."

"I do," I confirmed. He drove to the facility. "Oliver, are you healed?" I asked as he parked.

"Yeah." He helped me carefully across the swamp.

"Andrea, Ollie, how was school," Ric asked.

"Glad it's over," I replied stiffly. I knew I was being rude but I couldn't focus on anything other than my dad.

"Get some weapons. We're going to the basement." I grabbed my sword and followed Ric. Alex and Eli were standing guard in front of the door. "Andrea, stay next to Ollie."

"Why, what are we doing?"

"We're going to knock out the prisoners and cuff them. We have to be able to pull them out with chains."

"Who's knocking them out?" I asked.

"I am," Celine said, stepping in front of me. We went in and she looked around the room with her eagle-sharp eyes. She took out her gun and shot into the dark, three times. We heard three bodies hitting the floor in quick succession.

"Great work," Ric complimented. He and Alex walked into the dark. I drew my sword, ready for anything. We heard clicking sounds moments later.

"Andrea, Eli, catch," Ric called. Chains came flying out and I caught them. "Attach them to the stair railings." We did.

"Done!" I called back nervously. Ric and Eli came back out. "Did you do it?" I asked breathlessly.

"Yeah," Ric confirmed, wrapping an arm reassuringly around me. "We can pull them out using the chains. Come up to the war council."

We went to the conference room. I watched in awe as everyone stood up when Ric and I walked into the room. Everyone, including Ric, waited to sit until I did.

"We secured the Dokkalfar," he began confidently. "I'll take our best troops to bring them with us. My mother, our alpha, Lilian Velvela will be returning to us. I need the elders to arrange the funeral rites for her. We also need to bring her home with dignity. Eli, Celine, Alex, Oliver, Andrea, and I will cover that. Andrew and Lise, be sure to keep all of your teams away from the bridge tonight. I don't want any more human casualties. Troops have to be equipped with sufficient weaponry."

"What kind of funeral arrangements do you want?" someone asked.

"I want a funeral fit for an alpha. If there are no other questions, you're dismissed," he concluded with the same level of confidence. I supposed being an alpha meant that he could never really display his true feelings publicly.

"That's it, Ric. I need Andrea," Celine said. He nodded and Celine dragged me with her.

"Where are we going?" I asked.

"I have something for you." She led me into her room and shut the door. She showed me a pitch-black sports bra.

"Umm, Celine, I already have bras," I said, embarrassed.

"It's embedded with armor and it's bulletproof," she defended validly, her eyes wide and trustworthy.

"Ohh, thanks," I said unsure of how exactly to pull off a bulletproof bra. "How do I wear this?"

"Like this," she pulled off her T-shirt. "I wear this and jeans in combat."

"Okay, you can pull off anything with a body like yours," I complimented.

"Go try it on," she pushed. I went to her bathroom and put it on over my jeans. I went out boldly. I wasn't very self-conscious. "That's a good look on you. You look like a warrior princess." I laughed at her and she handed me a few more pieces. My phone rang as I went downstairs.

"Andie, where are you?" Jack asked, concerned.

"I'm at the facility," I soothed.

"Do you need me to come over?"

"No, thanks, Jack. I'll call you if something comes up."

I spent the evening working with the weapons. I was making sure I was comfortable in my armor and that I could move freely.

"Andrea, come get something to eat," Celine called a while later. I took Freya from her and grabbed a sandwich. Ric came up behind us as we sat at a table.

"Why don't I hold the baby while you girls eat?" he offered. I carefully handed over Celine's daughter.

"Andrea," he began conversationally, "Can you watch Freya in a couple of days? I wanted to take her mother out to dinner. If she says yes, that is."

"Really, Ric, that's how you ask me out?" Celine said, beaming despite how Ric phrased his question.

"Sorry. I'm winging it. What do you say?"

"Of course go, if Andrea babysits."

"Sure, Celine. I'll take her."

"You girls should get dressed after dinner," Ric said. Celine and I looked at each other.

"Umm, Ric, we are dressed. This is it," Celine stated.

"Okay. I'll have someone bring your robes. You'll need them to bring mother home. Andrea, you'll be taking point. The Dokkalfar know about our matriarchal ways. Oliver and I will flank you. You'll be safe."

"I have to lead our army?" I demanded in shock. I wasn't ready for such a huge responsibility. I was just learning how to be a wolf. There was no way I could be the alpha.

"They have to think you're leading us. I'll help you," he soothed. I took a deep breath. "Celine, can you help her with her armor?"

"She already has some on, Ric. It's the armor I designed."

"The war helmet at least." I had no idea what they were talking about. I figured they would tell me soon enough.

"That one?" Celine speculated.

"Yes. It's time," Ric affirmed.

I couldn't wait any longer. "Which one?" I asked.

"Our mother's. It's part of the alpha's war regalia and is yours now."

"I'll show you," Celine intervened. We went to the top floor of the facility. She used a code to let us into the room. There was a glass case at the end of the room. I gasped in awe as I saw the armor it held. It looked like gold and obsidian. There was a breastplate, helmet, weapon holders, and two pairs of beautiful combat boots. The craftsmanship was extraordinary. I could see that a lot of effort and time was put into making this masterpiece. Celine used another code to open the case.

"Why doesn't Ric wear this?" I asked, unable to understand why someone would refuse to wear this outstanding creation.

"The most obvious reason is that it's a woman's armor and also, it's yours." After a closer look, I realized that the breastplate was suited for a woman's body. She took out the helmet.

"Can I have the boots too?" I blurted, unable to stop myself. They were magnificent.

"Sure," she took out a pair and we went back down. I put on the boots, they were calf-length, and we went to the armory. I put blades in my boots and took my sword. I put a gun in its holster. Celine brought me a bow and quiver.

"I already have a lot of weapons on me," I protested.

"This is symbolic. It's for the alpha."

"The alpha has a lot to worry about," I noted, exasperated. A part of me was also worried that I wouldn't be able to handle all of this.

"She does, but you don't. Ric will never force you into stepping up. He'll cover for you as long as you need him to. That's one of the best things about your brother." I took the bow and shouldered the quiver.

"Are you ready?" Ric asked, coming in. Celine nodded in assent. "Andrea, don't let your emotions show tonight. Whatever happens." I wasn't sure what I was feeling. My dad was coming back to me, but he had been taken hostage by the same creatures who murdered my mom. I wasn't sure what state he would be in when I got him back. I grabbed the helmet and went to the main hall, where everyone was gathered. Celine disappeared with a knowing glance toward Ric.

"Tonight treat Andrea as the alpha. The Dokkalfar have to know that we have an actual alpha. You'll also be receiving orders from me since Andrea doesn't know all of our battle strategies yet. I need all of you to cover her." Celine returned with some wolves trailing her. Someone brought Ric his armor, which he strapped on quickly.

We walked to the bridge. "Andrea, stay with the wolves. Come to the front when I signal you to."

"How do I know what the signal is?"

"You'll know," he assured. "Alex, guard her. Stay close to her. You'll be presenting her. Ollie, you and I will be on point until she's presented. Celine, you'll flank me. Eli, you're with Ollie. The hostages will be behind Andrea," he whispered hurriedly. We positioned ourselves according to his orders.

Alex drew his sword and swept the terrain. I felt the wolves behind me and I could hear the Dokkalfar's chains rattling behind them. Oliver and Ric stood in front of us. A few troops separated us. I saw Celine and Eli with their weapons ready. We walked across the bridge, to the middle.

"Our king," one of the Dokkalfar began. I felt a chill run down my spine as he spoke. His voice sounded like nails grating on a blackboard. "King Ira." One of them took point. He had extra armor and commanded respect, the king of the Dokkalfar.

"Where is your leader?" he demanded dryly, obviously knowledgeable about our pack leadership.

"I'm honored to present our alpha, Andrea," Ric replied. Alex offered me his arm formally and I took it. The troops parted to make way for us. I noticed that they all were in attention, keeping an eye out for any sign of trouble. I let him walk me forward. I felt paws plodding behind me, Orion. He let go of me behind Oliver and Ric and I continued to walk forward. I stopped a few feet in front of them, between both of them. Orion stood right behind me.

"It's a pleasure to meet the alpha. Where are the princes?" he inquired in his menacing voice. "Behind us," I replied as confidently as I could. If I let Ric speak for me, it would cause doubt in the king.

"I want confirmation before I hand over Lilian and Nicolas's corpses."

"Nicolas's corpse?" I asked, trying to stay calm. I remembered Ric's warning not to show any emotion.

"Ahh, Yes. He succumbed to his injuries. We have him in a coffin too," Ira replied as if that were a great service. I worked hard to push my emotions aside. I could feel waves of tension rolling off Ric.

"How long have you had him?" I asked in what I thought was a conversational tone.

"Over a week. The princes," he repeated, demanding this time. Ric barked an order and a commander dragged the three elves forward.

"The coffins," I demanded. Some of the elves wheeled two coffins forward. They stopped in front of their king. One was simple and plain while the other was decorated. The Dokkalfar troops turned in synchronization and marched away.

12

I felt something shatter inside me. The emotions I had been holding back. At that moment, I knew what emotion triggered my transformation. Heartbreaking, nerve-racking grief to the highest degree. It was also what brought me back to my senses when I was a wolf. I changed back as soon as I thought I had hurt Jack.

I turned around and collapsed onto the cold tar ground before anyone could catch me. The wolf burst out and I was on all fours. All my weapons clanged onto the ground. I ran to the facility and bounded up to my room. I felt another set of paws following me. They stopped outside my room. From the thoughts, I recognized that it was Orion. I knew I had expectations to meet. I couldn't let myself break down this way.

I knew my dad would want me to put on a good face. I struggled to turn human again. I dressed in fresh armor and jeans. I took a minute to compose myself. I snuck out of the facility and drove a jeep back to the path to the bridge. The troops hadn't left yet. Ric was probably contemplating whether I would come back or not. I went to stand next to Ric. I could feel how blank my face was. He put his arm around me carefully.

"I'm so sorry, Andrea," he lamented. I couldn't afford to feel anything now. I pretended like I hadn't heard him.

"Let's bring her home," I said blandly. Someone handed me a robe and I pulled it over myself. I tied the robe tightly and pulled my hood up, letting it hide my face. Ric and I stood at the front of Lilian's coffin. Celine and Oliver were in the middle while Eli and Alex were at the back. They all wore black robes identical to mine. We hoisted her coffin onto her shoulders. I noticed some commanders carrying my dad's coffin. Like pallbearers, we carried her on our shoulders to the cove and across the swamp. Everyone stood up as a sign of respect as we carried the coffin through the facility. We laid her coffin in the hall of alphas. The top of the coffin was transparent. I could see her. Her body was perfectly preserved. She was beautiful, or rather mesmerizing.

The commanders brought my dad's coffin in and laid it next to Lilian's. I turned away from it. I couldn't bear to think of my dad. I thought he was away for work when in reality he was being tortured. My heart felt like it had shattered. Dad and I were all each other had left. I was all alone now.

"Excuse me," I muttered and ran to my room. I shut the door and pulled off my robe. I threw myself on the bed and let the tears flow freely. There was a knock on my door a while later. I didn't reply. It opened and closed again. Someone sat next to me and rubbed my arm, trying to soothe me.

"Andie," came Jack's voice, full of sorrow. I turned around, my face wreathed in tears. He took one look at me and enfolded me in his arms. My head rested on his chest and he rubbed my back, trying desperately to calm me down.

"I don't have anyone anymore," I sobbed, my tears ruining his thin T-shirt. I was finding it hard to breathe through my tears. I was pretty much choking my words out.

"You have me, Andrea. You always will," he promised. "Your brother is waiting outside. Can he come in?" he asked after a few moments passed. A part of me registered that Jack didn't know how to handle the situation any more than I did.

I nodded and soon felt another pair of arms around me. "Andrea, I'm your family now," Ric vowed. I cried even harder in the arms of the brother I'd known for a week. "Andrew and Lise will take care of your dad. He'll have an honorable funeral from the FBI." The words sounded so weird. Nothing about my dad's death was honorable.

"What about Lilian?" I asked, hollow.

"Her funeral will be in a few days. People are coming from out of state."

"Andie, try to get some sleep. I'll be right here." Ric left and Jack laid next to me. I felt safe and comfortable next to him. There was nothing awkward about lying next to Jack.

The next morning, I went to the dining room in the morning. Andrew and Lise came up to me. "We're so sorry, Andrea. We'll make the arrangements and someone will email you. They'll ask you to come to the headquarters. They'll also ask you for a legal guardian. You can bring Ric."

I nodded silently. I took a glass of orange juice and sat down. "Can you drive me to school?" I asked Ric.

"You want to go to school today?" he asked, amazed.

"Yes. Can you drive me?"

"I don't know if you should go to school today. You were just introduced as the alpha."

"I don't care. I'm going, even if I have to walk," I said stubbornly.

"No, I'll take you. Get ready," he accepted.

I showered and dressed in jeans, an armored bra, and a low-necked T-shirt. I went downstairs and found Jack and Oliver at the exit. Ric had brought my car up front. I got in the passenger seat.

"Andrea, I'll be on call if you need me. Please, let me know if you need me," Ric pleaded, his eyes wide and genuine as he pulled into the parking lots.

"I'll be fine," I said, my voice emotionless. He looked at me with concern. He brushed my hair back gently and I got out of the car. I went straight to my first class, ignoring all the waves and smiles directed at me. I sat at the back of the room and tried to focus. I couldn't do it. I put my head on the desk and cried. I felt like my heart was being squeezed and I'd been trying not to show it. I had been trying to put on a good face. I didn't realize how loud my sobs were. The teacher was tapping my shoulder.

"Ms. Morgan, are you okay?" I nodded without looking up. "Look at me, Andrea," she said more gently.

I looked up at her, not bothering to compose myself and Jack rushed over. He inserted himself between us and hugged me, discreetly turning my face into his shoulder.

"Your eyes," he breathed in my ear.

"Mr. Russell, what's wrong with her?" the teacher asked, concerning coloring her voice. I tried to pull my wolf eyes back. I stood up abruptly and looked at the floor.

"Excuse me," I murmured.

"I'll take care of her," Jack promised and followed me out. I rushed to the gym and crumpled limply in the middle of the floor, in a fetal position. "Andie, do you need me to get Ric?"

"No," I said, my teeth gritted. I was trying not to let the wolf out. I felt my phone buzz in my pocket. I took it out to read the message I had received. "It's from the FBI, Jack. They want me to come to headquarters."

"Do you want me to come?"

"No. I'll take Ric. Thanks, Jack. Tell the coach where I am and have Allison lead cheer practice. I'll text you when I know more," I assured and called Ric.

"Andrea, what's wrong?"

"The FBI texted me, Ric. I have to go see them. Can you come?"

"Of course. I'm at the facility. Come here, get changed and we can go." I hung up and picked myself up off the floor. Jack stood too and opened his arms to me. I accepted without hesitation. He hugged me and kissed my hair gently. I was so grateful for the platonic love Jack and I shared. Our bond had no equivalent. He searched my eyes for a second before letting me go wordlessly. I went to my car and Oliver caught me.

"Where are you going?" he demanded.

"To the FBI," I answered simply. I wasn't really sure how I felt about him yet. I understood that he was my mother's son and I could tell that he loved me unconditionally. It wasn't as strong as what I had with Jack, obviously, but I could feel his intensity. I was good enough at reading people to tell it wasn't romantic.

Oliver let me go and I got into my car. I drove to the facility and went to my room. I dressed in a thigh-length, navy blue dress. I put on my necklace and put on a pair of neat pumps. I brushed my hair into a 'messy' bun at the nape of my neck. I put my phone in a purse and went to Ric's room.

"Are you ready?" he asked.

"Yeah. Let's go." We went back to my car and Ric drove to the headquarters. After the guards frisked us, we were led to the receptionist.

"Name and business," he asked brusquely.

"I'm Andrea Morgan. Nicolas's daughter. I received a text asking me to come here."

"Ms. Morgan, the director is expecting you. Follow me." He led us up to the top floor. "Wait here until he calls you in."

Ric and I sat on the couch. His arm automatically encircled me protectively. "Come in, Ms. Morgan," a man called. Ric and I opened the door and we saw Lise in the room with another man. "Andrea, I've heard so much about you. I'm Director Doherty. Please sit down. Who's this?"

"I'm her stepbrother, Ric."

"I wasn't aware Nicolas had another child," the director said inquisitively.

"I'm his wife's firstborn son, sir."

"Nick never mentioned you."

"After my mom died I was raised by my extended family, sir. I never met Nicolas. All I knew was that my mother told me to look after my little sister."

The director nodded, satisfied with Ric's explanation, and turned to me. "Andrea, I have some upsetting news about Nicolas," the director said after nodding at Ric. I braced myself and Ric took my hand under the table. "Our agents found him dead when he should have been working on a case."

The way he said it made me feel like this was my fault. My dad would be alive if I wasn't his daughter. It was because I was a wolf that he had been taken and tortured and killed. This revelation brought fresh tears to my eyes. Ric squeezed my arm as I fought to stay in control of myself.

"I'm sorry, Ms. Morgan. You'll receive your father's salary as a pension every month. The state will pay for your educational needs. We will be organizing a funeral for this Friday. This envelope has your father's salary for this month. Ms. Morgan, you will be put in the foster system as you don't have any legal guardians.

"I can be her guardian," Ric intervened quickly. "I can't have my sister in foster care."

"How old are you?"

"I'm 25 years old, sir."

"Are you sure that you can be responsible for Andrea Morgan?"

"I will."

"Andrea, do you accept?" Anything would be better than the foster system. I could do a lot worse than Ric. I was glad that it was him and not anyone else in his place. I nodded.

"Okay. It's settled. Mr. Ric, you will need to sign some papers and visit Andrea's school, establishing yourself as her guardian." I wasn't sure how the adoption process worked. Maybe as the director of the FBI, Doherty had the power to grant adoptions.

"I'll do that, sir," Ric said and then filled out a few legal forms.

"Andrea, please feel free to come to me if you ever need anything," the director said as we were leaving.

"Thank you," I replied.

Ric and I went to my car. "Andrea, I'll move into your apartment as soon as Mom's funeral is over. I promise I'll be an attentive and responsible brother."

"Thanks," I said, feeling an emotion other than grief for the first time since last night. It was gratitude. I hoped he could read that in my voice.

"Why don't we head to your school? I'll talk to your principal and then we can go to the facility."

"Okay." I showed him to the principal's office and then went to the soccer field to watch practice. I sat on the bottom of the bleachers.

"Morgan! Where's your jersey? What are you doing in that getup?" coach demanded.

"I'm just here to watch," I explained. He pretended not to hear me.

"Get in here," he ordered. I took off my heels and ran in. I jumped and flipped, kicking the ball. I landed lightly on my feet.

"You're late. You're not dressed. You look like you're headed to a fancy conference. What are you doing?" he asked.

"I was at the FBI headquarters. I thought Jack told you."

"He did. I want to know why?" he pressed. He was going to make me say the words out loud.

"My dad died on duty. They talked to me about it. I came back here to introduce my brother to the principal as my legal authority."

"I'm sorry to hear that," he said, for once in a voice that wasn't a shout.

"Andrea," Ric called from the edge of the field.

"Coach, that's my brother," I informed, waving Ric over.

"Hi. I'm Ric, Andrea's step-brother and legal guardian. Andrea, are you ready to leave?"

"Yeah. I'll see you tomorrow coach."

"Andrea, there's a game tomorrow," the coach reminded.

"I'll be there, coach, I assured. I waved goodbye to Jack and left with Ric. We drove to the facility in silence. Things were in full swing there.

"What's going on?" I asked.

"They are getting ready for the funeral," he explained.

"When is it?"

"The day after tomorrow. Thursday."

"Okay," I said, making a mental note of it in my mind.

"You have a dress code, Andrea. Celine will get you the dress."

"Ric, I'm not a dress person."

"You look great in them, Andrea. I think. I haven't seen you in a full dress."

"Where's Celine," I surrendered,

"She should be up in her room with Freya." I went upstairs and knocked on Celine's door.

"Come in... hey, Andrea. How was the FBI?"

"Ric's my legal guardian now. Speaking of Ric, did you two plan your date yet?"

"He thinks we should wait," she said solemnly.

"Why?"

"He wants to make sure you're okay. He told me he's going to move in with you."

"He is," I confirmed. "I'll make sure he asks you after my dad's funeral."

"Thanks, Andrea. So, what's up? Are you here for your funeral dress?"

"Should I brace myself?" I asked warily.

"Oh, Nonsense." She gave me Freya and went into her walk-in closet. She brought out a long black dress. She turned it so I could see it from all directions. It was backless and looked tight to the waist. It didn't look like it had a lot of volume.

"Not bad," I noted.

"It's heavy velvet and there's a veil that goes with it."

"Wait, it's not a zombie bride costume right?"

"No. It's this old belief that the aura of the dead sticks to people. The veil protects the next alpha from being affected."

"Ohh. If you say so," I shrugged.

"Do you want to try it on so I can see if it needs to be altered?"

I nodded and put Freya in her crib. I took the dress and changed in the bathroom. Celine walked around me, inspecting the dress.

"It's a perfect fit," she declared. I changed into clothes I could train in and went downstairs. I hung up a punching bag and wrapped my hands. I started attacking the bag furiously then moved on to a wooden dummy, using two blades against it.

"Ahh!" I exclaimed, vaulting over it. Someone touched me from behind and I spun around, my blades slashing wildly.

"Andrea, it's Alex. Calm down," a voice said, grabbing my arms in a quick movement.

"Oh my god, Alex! Did I hurt you?"

"No. I'm the best in the pack at defense."

"You all have some unique talent," I commented. I had been picking up on what everyone said about my new friends. "Celine is the best shooter. Oliver is a pro at blade combat. No one can beat Ric in hand-to-hand combat. Eli is the best strategist. What do I do?" I asked, feeling like I wasn't very important to the pack.

"I've been watching you, Andrea. You'll best us all if you keep training. Let me join you. Try to defend against me."

"What do you use for defense?"

"It depends on your technique, Andrea."

"Well, I don't know what my technique is," I admitted.

"I do. You use a perfectly balanced sword, Andrea. That signifies a need for balance in your fighting techniques. You need balance to be effective. Use a sword and a shield. I'll start slow."

"Do I need a shield?" I asked. I wasn't sure I was comfortable with a shield.

"You could defend with two blades, but you'll have more balance with a shield. Try it. You can change to blades later if you want to."

I nodded and took a shield. I drew my sword from my belt and faced Alex.

"Remember, Andrea. You're on defense. Don't attack me." I nodded again and he took out his sword. I focused on not attacking and tried to anticipate his moves before he made them. I could tell he was going slowly to give me a decent chance. I tried to use the shield but I wasn't sure what to do with it.

"Cover your head and chest, Andrea."

"Isn't that why I'll have a helmet and armor?"

"You can never have too much protection." We continued for half an hour.

"Alex, dinner," Eli called. "Andrea, can I have a word with you?"

"Sure." I put my sword in the rack and hung up the shield.

"I haven't had a chance to ask how you were doing," he admitted.

"I'm not sure. I have no idea what I'm doing," I informed calmly.

"I'm here for you, Andrea. We all are. Do you know what Ric's doing now?"

"What?"

"Getting ready to move. He's going to take you home after dinner."

"He said it would be after Mom's funeral."

"He thinks it would be better if you were in familiar surroundings. I spent the day boxing up your dad's things."

"Really? Thanks. I never asked, where's your family?"

"We don't talk, Andrea. My dad was Lilian's stepbrother. They were really close once. He was her most trusted advisor. Lilian is said to have taken a heather bullet for him. They fought over something and he left. I decided to stay. I haven't talked to him in over ten years. I don't even know if he'll come to the funeral."

"So we're related?" I asked.

"Not by blood," he laughed.

"What about Alex?"

"His mom was Lilian's best friend and his dad was her high school sweetheart. They died in the war with the Dokkalfar."

"I'm sorry," I said blandly.

"It was all years ago. We should go now." Ric tapped my shoulder after dinner.

"Andrea, do you want to go home tonight? I have my things ready."

"That would be really nice, Ric. Thanks. I'll go grab a bag."

I went to my room and gathered some of my things and went out to my car. My phone rang.

"Hey, Jack."

"Andie, where are you?"

"I'm leaving the facility to go home. Ric is coming with me."

"Will you be in school tomorrow?"

"I should be Jack. How was practice?"

"Soccer was the same as usual. I sprained my wrist in cheer practice."

"Oh my god Jack. Are you okay?"

"Yeah, Andie. The doc says I can't use it for a week."

"What were you trying to do? Who was spotting you?"

"No one wanted to spot me, so I did it myself."

"Jack, I should have been there," I lamented. I was furious about the prejudice that everyone had about Jack.

"I'll be fine. I'll see you tomorrow." Ric was in the car already. There were boxes of his stuff in the back. I got in and he started driving.

"Has there been any sign of the Dokkalfar?"

"There haven't been any homicides in the past twenty-four hours, Andrea. But, we aren't going to let our guard down." When we got home, I silently went to my room and fell asleep.

13

I walked out of my room the next morning, feeling well-rested.

"Good morning, Andrea. Come have breakfast."

"Did you make something, Ric?" I asked.

"I did. Come on."

I sat at the table and my phone rang. "Andie, can you come to pick me up?"

"Sure, Jack. I'll be there in a few."

"Where are you going?" Ric asked.

"To get Jack before school. I have a game this evening. I'll be staying at school after classes with the rest of the team."

"I'll come watch the game," he promised.

"That sounds great." I scarfed down my cereal and went to my car. I threw my bag in the backseat and drove to Jack's/ he was waiting outside his apartment.

"How's your arm?" I demanded.

"It doesn't hurt anymore, but I can't play tonight."

"What were you trying to do yesterday?"

"I don't know what they called it, Andie."

"Jack, I'm so sorry. I should have been there to make sure you would be okay."

"It's not your fault, Andie." Jack went directly to class and I called an emergency cheer meeting under the bleachers.

"Allison, you were supposed to be in charge yesterday. Now we have an injured soccer player."

"It's not her fault that he got hurt," Katie defended.

"I'm not talking to you right now. Allison, it was your responsibility to make sure they were spotted. Wait, hold on. This is actually on all of you. Couldn't one of you spot Jack? I don't understand what you all have against him. This is your final warning." I turned on my heel and marched to class.

"What's up?" Jack asked as I sat next to him.

"I just had to put some people in their place." Oliver walked by me and discreetly slipped a note in my hand. 'Can we talk?' it read.

"Jack, I'll be back in a few," I went to the gym and Oliver came in minutes later.

"What's wrong?" I asked him.

"I wanted to ask you that Andrea. Are you upset with me?"

"Not right now. Why?" I asked, puzzled. I was being honest. I didn't have it in me to be mad at anyone now.

"You haven't really talked to me."

"If you think I was ignoring you, I wasn't."

"Then why didn't I get an invitation to your home? You've known Ric for two weeks and me for years. I thought you'd trust me."

"It's not that I don't trust you, Oliver. I thought you'd have your own place. You don't live at the facility, do you?"

"I'm in the foster system again, Andrea. After Lilian died they took me back. When she passed, Ric was too young to be my guardian. I don't live in the facility. I live in a godforsaken orphanage. I don't have any family. I hoped you'd me my family. Someone who'd love me unconditionally. Why else do you think I followed you around for years? I know so much about you, Andrea, maybe even more than Jack."

All that information was a bit too much for me to process. I didn't know what to say. I could hear the truth ringing in his voice.

"Oliver, I'm so sorry. I didn't know," I said hurriedly. The bell rang, interrupting us. He got up and left the gym. At that moment I knew Oliver was as much my brother as Ric was. My mother loved him and he loved me. Wasn't that criteria enough? I was determined to show him that I accepted him. No, that wouldn't be enough. It wasn't only acceptance he sought. He wanted love. I called Ric.

"Andrea, are you okay?"

"I am. Do you know the orphanage Oliver lives in?"

"Of course I do," he said, confused.

"What do you think about being responsible for another teenager?"

"Who are you talking about?"

"Oliver. Will you be his legal authority?"

Ric didn't hesitate for a second before replying, "I will."

"Come pick me up. We're going over there now."

Ric and I were at the orphanage in an hour.

"Please, come in. I'm Mrs. Rose," a stout woman said, "Head of the institution. How can I help you folks?"

"Is there somewhere we can talk?" Ric asked.

"My office. Follow me... What can I do for you?"

"I'm Ric Velvela. My mother was Lilian. She fostered a boy who was taken in here after her death, Oliver West."

"Yes, we took him after Lilian died," she confirmed.

"He was like a brother to me and we remained close even after Lilian's passing. I'd like to become his legal guardian."

"I'm sorry sir, are you offering to foster him?"

"I'm saying I'd like to adopt him as my brother."

"Ohh. That's wonderful!" she gushed. "He's at school right now but you can finish up the paperwork."

"Of course," Ric agreed.

"And who might you be, young lady?"

"I'm Andrea Morgan, Ric's stepsister."

Ric filled out all the necessary documents. "We'll come back later tonight," he said. He drove me back to school, just in time for cheer practice. I pulled on my uniform and rushed to the gym.

"I don't know what happened yesterday, but I want you all to know that it will never happen again. Do I make myself perfectly clear? I'll be on cheer today. Sophia, work with the soccer team."

"Andie, where were you?"

"I was with Ric. Take it easy," I reminded. After cheer, we went to the soccer field. I was still in my cheer uniform. I decided to change into my jersey before the game.

"Ms. Morgan, are you playing tonight?" the coach asked.

"You bet," I confirmed.

"Great. Boys, positions! You're going to try to score against our goalie. Defend Andrea. Liam pick a couple of guys and try to get the ball from her. Oliver, help her out. Get her to the goal, or better yet, she doesn't need to be near the goal. She just needs the ball. Russell, you're on the bench until you're healed."

I stood in the middle of the field as the ball rolled out. I was better at aerial shots. I cartwheeled and kicked the ball up. I flipped when it was flying and kicked it into the goal.

I went to the bleachers a few hours later. I laid my head on Jack's lap. "You're great out there," he complimented.

"Thanks, Jack. Uhh, I have to go get changed."

"Rest for a few minutes, Andie. You have been running around all day."

"It's not over yet, Jack." I went to the locker room and dressed in my jersey. I went to the air-conditioned gym and saw Oliver and Liam on the bleachers. I was about to walk out when Liam stood up.

"Hey, Andrea. Why were you at the FBI office yesterday?"

"Why do you care?"

"I'm just trying to be nice," he defended.

"No thanks."

"I see I'm not welcome here," he said, leaving. I waited until he was out of sight before sitting down next to Oliver, looking at my entwined fingers.

"Hey," I said.

"Hey," he muttered.

"I'm really sorry about this morning. I didn't know," I apologized, trying to put a lot of emotion into the words.

"I know Andrea. There was no way you could have known."

"Does anyone else know?"

"The administration, teachers, guys on the team, Liam," he stated.

"I promise, we'll talk about this later. Come on." I knew it wasn't much, but I wanted to surprise him. I squeezed his shoulder gently and stood up. We went to the field and I tied my hair up, ready for action. We won the game in the final minutes. After the game, I went to Ric. He was talking to Oliver.

"I have to leave, Ric. I got a phone call asking me to come back," Oliver was saying.

"I thought you and Liam were hosting the victory party," I thought out loud.

"He can take care of it on his own," Oliver said, leaving.

I said a hurried goodbye to Jack before we left for the orphanage.

Mrs. Rose came bustling over to greet us. "Please, wait right here. I told Oliver he was being adopted and that his family was on their way. He's so excited to meet you. I'll ask him to hurry up."

"It's fine, we can wait," I assured, realizing that I should have changed into something more presentable. I could feel sweat drying on my back. We waited in the entrance hall for about fifteen minutes.

"Come on, Oliver," Mrs. Rose was saying, "hurry up."

"I'm coming," he replied.

Oliver turned around the corner and stopped in his tracks. "Hey," I said. He ran to us and threw his arms around me. "Ollie, I'm all sweaty and gross," I protested. He didn't pay any attention to my warning. He moved his arms to my waist and picked me up, spinning me. Ric joined us after Oliver set me down.

"We're your family now, brother," Ric said, ruffling his hair.

"Oliver, why don't you get your things?" Mrs. Rose suggested.

He let go of us and turned on his heel, only to complete the turn and face me again. He squeezed me one more time and then ran upstairs, yelling, "I'll be ready in a few."

"That's the happiest I've ever seen him. Thank you, Mr. Velvela."

"Please, call me Ric and it's my pleasure." He went upstairs to help Oliver. I sat down, crossing one leg over the other, smiling to myself.

"Andrea, can you bring your car up front?" Ric called a half hour later. I did and watched my brothers carry boxes downstairs. They loaded them into the trunk of the car.

"Are you ready to go?" I asked.

"Are we going to the facility?" Oliver wondered.

"Not exactly. Get in," I invited mysteriously. I drove to my apartment and Ric covered Oliver's eyes with a black cloth. I opened the car door and took his hands. "Come on," I said, leading him up. Ric opened the door to the apartment as I uncovered Oliver's eyes.

"Welcome home," I smiled. I watched his jaw drop as he took it all in.

"Andrea..." he breathed, shocked.

"Hold that thought, Ollie. Make yourself comfortable. I'll be back in a few minutes." I was filthy. I went to my room and showered quickly. I dressed up in a T-shirt and shorts. I went to the living room and sat on the couch, between Oliver and Ric.

"When did you two think of all this?" Oliver asked, still in shock.

"It was all Andrea," Ric provided.

"I don't know what to say," he said, looking at me. Heat rose to his cheeks, coloring them red.

"Consider it what I owe you for loving me for years," I said simply. We sat around chatting for a while. I fought off sleep every minute. Jack was right, I had been running around all day.

"Ric, what do you do all day?" I asked. I was genuinely curious. There was no way he just sat around all day at the facility.

"I run a company, Andrea. I'm the director of EclipseTech, the home appliances company."

"Wait. What?"

"I use an alias in public so no one can trace Ric Velvela to the director."

"You're Richard Venus?"

"I am."

"You own a huge estate in upstate New York?"

"I do. I live there when things are slow at the facility."

"You never mentioned that before!" I exclaimed.

"It never came up in a conversation. I'll take you both there sometime. I mean, we could move there if you want to."

"Ric, I don't know what to say," I said. It was my turn to be speechless.

"You don't need to answer immediately. We should all get to bed. We have a long day tomorrow." I stepped off the couch and staggered to bed. Tomorrow was Lilian's funeral. I would have to appear in front of the whole pack again. I had to be perfect. I had to be who they needed.

14

I woke up to knocking on my door. "Andrea, get up. We have to leave soon!" I rolled out of bed and staggered to the door, my hair flopping all over my face.

"Hey," I groaned.

"Andrea, shower and get dressed. Celine will help you into your funeral dress at the facility."

I dressed in a knee-length black dress and brushed my hair down. I put on some moonstones and stepped into gentle black stilettos. I put on some makeup and took my phone.

"Ric, Oliver, I'm ready," I called from the living room. They came out in matching tuxedoes.

"You will only have fifteen minutes to get ready, Andrea," Ric informed.

"No problem,"

We got into the car and Ric drove to the facility. Oliver helped me across the swamp. Ric formally offered me his arm before we entered. I took it and he led me inside. He walked me up to my room.

"Get ready, I'll be waiting for you downstairs." Celine was waiting to pounce.

"Come on, take off your dress," she rushed. I changed into the funeral dress. She quickly arranged my hair into a twist with my hair over my shoulder. She painted my face, neatly applying a layer of bright red lipstick. She carefully pinned the veil to my hair. She arranged it to cover my face. "Are you comfortable? Can you see? Does anything hurt?"

"Everything's perfect," I reassured her.

"Okay, then go down. The funeral is behind the facility. Ric will escort you. People have been paying their respects since dawn. You'll do the same and stand next to Ric for a few hours. Then she'll be buried and will invite everyone to the dining hall. You'll take off the veil and join them."

"I got it," I said. Ric was waiting outside the room.

"Andrea, watch your step," he said as he offered me his arm. I took it and found myself grateful for the support. The last thing I wanted to do was fall. He walked me out and we formally approached the crowd. Celine was a few steps behind us. Everyone stood up as I approached. I walked past them to my mother's coffin. I didn't know what to say. I didn't really remember her.

I touched the coffin tenderly. "You will be avenged, Mother," I swore. I moved to stand next to Ric. Alex and Eli stepped in front of me in synchronization. I wondered if they had practiced it before. They took the front of my veil, holding one end each, and pulled it back, exposing my face. I guess I wouldn't be in danger of the aura sticking to me anymore.

Hours later, soldiers with weapons came forward. They lifted the coffin and we all followed them. Ric made sure that I was on point, leading the procession. She was carried to the cemetery and laid on the ground. We watched as her coffin was buried.

"Please join me in the dining hall," I invited as everyone turned to go back inside. Someone helped me unpin my veil.

"Andrea," Oliver called.

"Go with him, Andrea. I'll be there in a few minutes," Ric instructed. I adjusted my dress and let Oliver escort me inside. I sat next to him. There was a buffet arranged but I wasn't very hungry. I took a glass of juice as a waiter brought some around.

"Can I get you anything else, mam? Some vodka or wine perhaps?"

"No thanks. I'm good."

I went upstairs after lunch. I changed into the dress I was in this morning. I washed my face, cleaning off as much makeup as I could. I ponytailed my hair and traded my heels for boots. My phone rang.

"Hey, Andie. How was the funeral?"

"It's over, Jack. Tomorrow is my dad's. It's at the FBI headquarters. Will you come with me?"

"Of course I will. The coach was looking for you. I covered for you and told him you'd be out tomorrow too."

"Great."

"Do you want me to come over?"

"There are a lot of werewolves here that I might have to meet. It would be too dangerous for you to come here."

"Okay. I get it. I'll see you tomorrow." I hung up and went outside. Ric was waiting at the stairs.

"There are a lot of people waiting to meet you. Are you ready to go down?"

"I am," I confirmed. He handed me my sword and walked me around the facility. I met a lot of influential people. There were top businessmen, contractors, lawyers, doctors, and real estate owners. They all looked at me with so much respect, it was almost reverence. They were all older than me. It put me off balance. By 8 p.m. I was in the war council room. I was at the head of the table and the room was empty. My head dropped onto my shoulder out of exhaustion. I heard the door open and then close.

"Andrea," came Oliver's voice.

"Mmm..." I groaned in reply.

"Come on. Let's get you home." I felt my arm being pulled over his shoulder. "Ric has the car up front." He pulled me to my feet but I was unsteady. "Hold on. Sit back down." He set me down. Keeping his left arm around me. He took off my high heels, holding them in his right hand. He moved the arm behind my knees and picked me up.

"Oliver..." I muttered.

"It's me, Andrea." I didn't protest as he carried me into the night. He put me in the back seat of the car and got in with me. I jerked up as the car started.

"Wh? Where?" I asked, disoriented.

"Hey, it's Oliver. We're going to your apartment."

"Where are my shoes?"

"I've got them. Relax." I let my head rest on Oliver's shoulder. Ric helped me up to my room and shut the door behind himself. I dropped my dress and fell asleep in my underwear.

I woke up, alert and rested, an hour before sunrise. I took a relaxing bubble bath and then washed my hair. I drained the tub and sat on the edge, blow-drying my hair. I dressed in a short, backless, black dress that was held up by lace. I put on some makeup and my moonstone ring. I put on strappy high heels. I sat on the couch with a few pieces of toast. Ric joined me a few minutes later. He would be coming to the funeral with me while Oliver would be in school.

"Are you ready to leave?" Ric asked me.

"As ready as I'll ever be," I admitted uneasily. Today would be harder than yesterday. We drove to Jack's house. He was ready and was waiting for us. I was nervous and fidgety.

The headquarters were buzzing with agents. They directed us to the hall. The director was there. "Ms. Morgan, you look lovely. Please, have a seat. We were waiting for you."

"Are we late?"

"No, you're on time. We are early."

The funeral went on without needing much help from me. I sat there as everyone paid their last respects to my dad and expressed their sorrow to me. After everyone was done, I stood up. Jack shadowed me as I went to my dad's coffin. I looked at him one last time.

We were back home by 10 p.m.

"How did it go?" Oliver asked as I walked in.

"It was longer than I expected," I said simply. I didn't feel like talking to anyone so I went to my room and changed for the night. I was in a thin tank top and shorts. My sword rested on the bedside table.

15

I could tell it wasn't morning when I woke up. Something felt wrong. I brushed the hilt of my sword with my fingers as I slipped out of bed. I opened the door of my room as the first bullet hit. The window of my room shattered in moments. I grabbed my phone and ran to the living room. Ric and Oliver came bursting out of their rooms.

"Andrea! Get down!" Ric ordered. Bullets started flying in.

I screamed and Ric and Oliver both threw themselves in front of me, pushing me to the ground. I wrapped my arms around them, pulling them down with me. The boys were dead weight on me. The firing stopped for a split second. I pushed them off me and flipped over them, running to my room. I grabbed my car keys and my sword. The firing started again. Ric and Oliver were on the ground, bleeding profusely. I swung my sword around, deflecting the bullets. I grabbed Ric's blade and used it to shield us better. I saw Ric trying to stand.

"Andrea," he groaned.

"Hold on Ric," I pleaded. I continued to deflect the bullets until they paused again. I pulled Ric to his feet. He was weak but could balance stand on his own. I heaved Oliver up. He groaned unconsciously. The bullets had gone directly through his body. I dragged Oliver downstairs, making sure Ric was following. I laid Oliver in the back seat and helped Ric in. I threw my weapons in and drove, barefooted to the facility. I called Eli as I drove.

"Andrea, are you okay?"

"There was an attack on my apartment. Ric's hurt and Oliver's unconscious. I'm on my way to the facility."

"Are they healing?"

"I don't think so," I panicked.

"It's Heather and Wolfsbane. Hurry up. Are you hurt?"

"No, I was lucky." I hung up and the car whined as I accelerated.

Eli and Alex were waiting at the swamp with some medics. They took Ric out first. He groaned as they laid him on the stretcher. I helped them with Oliver. Every movement seemed to cause him pain.

"Shh. You'll be okay. I'm here," I said. I held his head as we rushed him to the infirmary. Someone cut Ric's shirt out of the way.

"Thank Sif, the blood is red," Celine breathed.

"What?" I asked.

"That means it's Heather. The wound will be cleaned and stitched up." The blood on Oliver's body was black. "This is Wolfsbane. It will have to be burned out."

Celine and Alex helped the doctors with Ric. The doctors had Oliver sit up. He was just regaining consciousness. I held him against me, sitting on the bed, his face buried in my shoulder. Eli was ready to hold him steady when he struggled. One of the doctors brought over a flame and some powder. They cut his ruined shirt off his body.

They coated his back with the powder, Oliver shrieked as the powder covered his wounds. I felt tears streak down my bare shoulder and neck. He bit me as the doctors used the flame to seal his wounds. Eli was about to pull his teeth out of my shoulder but I shook my head as I ran my blood-stained fingers through Oliver's hair. He started coughing violently as the doctors finished his back.

"Turn his head," Alex instructed, running over. I did and Oliver vomited a fountain of black goo.

"Turn him on his back," the doctor ordered. The wound has to be closed from both sides. I did, resting his head between my crossed legs. He gripped one of my arms and my bare thigh lightly. I placed my free hand firmly against his cheek.

"Arghh! It hurts!" he screamed.

"I know. I know. Just a little more, Ollie," I soothed. As the last wound was closed, he started coughing again. He coughed up blood this time, staining his face and my limbs red. His eyes closed and his body went limp in my arms.

"It's over. Shh... You're okay. That's it," I calmed. "Is Ric okay?"

"He's fine. It was just one bullet. He was lucky it was Heather. He's sleeping. Celine's with him," Alex said. "He asked about you. You're okay right?"

"I am. How long will it take for him to heal?" I asked, referring to Oliver as I touched his chest gently.

"A couple of days and they'll be fine." Oliver's eyes were still closed, his head on my lap. A nurse brought over a few pieces of cloth and warm water. He used them to start cleaning Oliver's body. He winced even in his sleep.

"Let me," I insisted, taking the cloth. I rubbed his cheek with my finger gently, my hair tickling him. I gently cleaned the blood off. He seemed to relax under my touch. I didn't move even after I was done. I watched him sleep. It was getting cold. Alex and Eli left. I pulled a blanket over him and felt the blood dry on my body. It was just before noon when his eyelids fluttered. His fingers twitched.

"Hey," I whispered, bending over him, my hair draping over his face

"That tickles," he breathed.

"Sorry," I laughed, pushing it back.

"Are you hurt?" he demanded with as much intensity as he could muster.

"No, you and Ric covered me."

"Why are you covered in blood?" he pressed.

"It's your blood, Ollie. Do you want to sit up?"

"I'm perfectly comfortable Andrea," he smiled.

"How do you feel?" I asked lamely.

"I don't know. I'll know when I sit up, I guess. Will you help me?"

"I thought you were comfortable," I teased before slipping off the bed without jostling him too much. I wasn't sure how to help him. He struggled to get up and I attempted to help. He sat up and closed his eyes.

"What's wrong?" I asked frantically. I put my arm around his shoulder to steady him.

"It's just the blood flowing, Andrea. Help me stand." I dropped my arm and he wound his over my shoulder. I was ready to catch him. He used me to pull himself up. His legs shook and I quickly sat him back down.

"Maybe we should take things more slowly," I suggested.

"Probably." I sat at the foot of the bed. "You're a mess, Andrea." I took a moment to visualize what I probably looked like. I was covered in dry blood from head to toe. My tank top and shorts were stained red. The ends of my amber hair were dyed red and black from the goo.

"It'll come off," I shrugged.

"Come here, Andrea." I moved closer and he wrapped his arms around me. I hugged him back.

"Andrea, he began, a different tone filling his voice.

"Yeah?"

"What's this on your shoulder?" I glanced at the shape of Oliver's teeth in my skin.

"Ohh, umm... you bit me last night," I explained.

"Oh my god. I'm so sorry," he lamented.

"It's okay. It'll heal soon." I brushed back his hair. "Will you be okay for a while? I'm going to drop in on Ric and clean up."

"Sure. Go ahead." I helped him lie down again and smiled at him before going to Ric. He was sitting in bed with Celine. His eyes popped when he caught sight of me.

"It's not mine," I assured, referring to the blood. I hugged him. "Why did you take that bullet for me?"

"I promised our mom I'd take care of you, Andrea. What kind of brother would it make me if I didn't protect you?"

"Thanks,"

"Andrea, I smell fresh blood."

"It must be from my shoulder," I reasoned.

"Are you injured?" he demanded.

"Oliver bit my shoulder when they burnt him."

"Is it deep? How long were his teeth in your body?"

"I'm not sure. Why?"

"The wound could become infected. You have to clean the wound and cover it up. Celine, check it."

Celine gingerly sniffed my shoulder. "I don't smell any bacteria, but you should go clean it up."

"Okay," I agreed immediately.

I went to my room and looked at myself in the mirror. I looked gruesome and macabre, there was no other way to say it. I showered, meticulously scrubbing all the blood off my body and my hair. I used rubbing alcohol to clean my shoulder. I covered it with a bandage and dried my hair, letting the hairdryer relax me.

I formulated a to-do list in my head. There would be cops at my apartment. I had to go back and smooth things over. I had to make sure my brothers were okay. I had to replace the broken windows and clean up. I dressed in jeans, armor, and a jacket. I stuck blades in my boots and put my sword in my belt. I marched back to the infirmary. Oliver was sitting up on the bed. I made sure my voice was tender when I spoke.

"Hey, Ollie,"

"You look like you're headed out."

"I am. I wanted to ask you something."

"Okay..."

"Why did you take those bullets for me?"

"I think that's obvious."

"Humor me," I pressed.

"I love you too much to let you get hurt," he whispered, his blue eyes meeting my emerald ones. He reached for me and I bent forward so he wouldn't have to stretch. He brushed my hair behind my ear with a gentleness that warmed my heart.

"Thanks," I smiled. "Rest. I'll be back in a few hours."

"Don't go out alone," he warned.

"I'm not. Don't worry," I assured as I went to hunt down Eli. "Are you free?" I inquired.

"What do you need?" he countered.

"I have to go to my place. I'm sure there are cops there by now."

"Sure, I'll take you. Let me go get my sword."

I went outside to wait for him. The sun's rays had managed to sneak through the thick foliage. I would need someone to clean the blood from my car. Eli went to get a jeep from the garage. I got into the passenger seat.

"How are you?" he asked, driving through Brooklyn.

"I'm okay. Ric and Oliver made sure of that."

"I'm glad you're okay." I was right. The apartment building was swarming with cops. I got out of the jeep with a backpack.

"Hey! Stop!" an officer ordered. "Who are you? What are you doing here?"

"I'm Andrea Morgan. My apartment was attacked sometime last night," I provided.

"Where did you spend your night?" he pressed.

"I went to my boyfriend's place."

"What about your parents?"

"My mom died when I was a child. My dad was the FBI agent Nicolas Morgan who just died."

The officer scrutinized me and then let us pass. My apartment was covered in yellow police tape. I grabbed my moonstone jewelry and stuffed it into my backpack. Eli grabbed the case of weapons from under my bed. I took some of my other personal belongings.

"What else do you need?" Eli asked.

"I need you to stay with me. There are people here to replace my windows and I need to clean up."

"Of course," he agreed.

I started cleaning after the window was replaced. I picked all the bullet casings up from the floor. "We'll take them to the facility. Our ballistics can try to match it," Eli said, taking them from me. I scrubbed the blood from the floor.

"Where to next?" Eli asked a few hours after I was done cleaning.

"The facility," I said.

"Will you be coming back here tonight?" he asked, concerned.

"I'm not sure," I admitted. We drove back to the facility. I had a guard take my things to my room. Everyone was on high alert. I went to the infirmary and found it empty. "Where are they?" I demanded to no one in particular.

"Ric is in his office, mam," a nurse told me. I nodded in acknowledgment and went to Ric's office.

"Andrea," he invited, sitting behind his desk.

"What are you doing? You're supposed to be resting!" I exclaimed.

"I'm alpha. We were attacked at our home. I have to tell people what to do. I already ordered a 24/7 guard and city-wide surveillance."

"Do you think it's the elves?" I asked.

"I'm open to all possibilities, Andrea."

"I can help, Ric."

"I know you can. I don't want to put all that on your shoulders yet."

"I can handle things," I protested.

"Okay,' he conceded. "You can work with the guards. They are yours to command."

I nodded. "I'll get on it. Where's Oliver?"

"He's in his room, probably asleep."

"I'll check on him and then go to the troops."

"Andrea, any wolf here will protect you, but I want you to have weapons on you."

"I will," I assured. I went up to my room. I traded my jacket for a knee-length leather coat. It was black and full-sleeved. It was kind of like a stylish bathrobe. There was a length of material I tied around my waist to give it a shape. The inside of the coat was filled with straps to hold blades. I strapped gun holsters to my thighs and ponytailed my hair high. I went to Oliver's room and knocked once.

"Ollie, it's Andrea," I announced, opening the door.

"Hey," he greeted.

"Did I wake you?"

"Of course not. Come in."

I went to him and perched on the bed. "How do you feel?"

"Andrea, this is nothing. I've had worse injuries. Where are you headed?"

"I'm going to speak with the guards."

"Let me get dressed, I'll join you."

"Take one day off, Ollie. I'll check on you later."

"I am tired," he admitted. "Did you get any sleep?"

"I'll get around to it," I said, leaving with a smile. I loaded up on weapons in the armory. I drew my sword and went out to the guards. I noticed two soldiers following me indiscreetly, obviously under Ric's order to keep me safe.

"I need everyone to stay alert. If anything happens, it comes to me first. Guard in shifts. Watch each other's backs.

A while after dusk, I heard screams and grunts. I was working out against a punching bag. I ran out to the main hall. Our soldiers were fiercely fighting against the Dokkalfar. They had taken down our guards. I was terrified but I steeled my nerves. I inhaled deeply and drew my sword. I flipped and slashed wildly.

I had to prove myself and protect my troops. I pulled out my gun and shot at the elves. I didn't wait to see if they hit their intended target. I knew I was making each bullet count. I threw my gun when it ran out of bullets. My pack was disorganized.

"Beta formation!" a clear, authoritative voice commanded. Ric was here. Everyone fell into perfectly organized groups, with me between them.

"Attack!" he called, drawing his blades. I assumed point and pulled blades from my boots, rolling forward in the same second. I skewered two elves and pulled the blades out. I saw the pack doing their best, but they were unprepared. Most of them were in casual clothes. They weren't ready for battle. My vision took on a red tinge.

"Cover your flanks!" I ordered. I was surprised to see my orders followed. I hacked my way through the elves' ranks. I barely noticed when a bullet entered my torso. I took off my coat, freeing my limbs.

"Cover her! Bring her back here!" Ric demanded.

"There are worse injuries, Ric," I replied. I fell as soon as I said that. A blade had run across my abdomen. I felt myself being dragged out of the way. Someone heaved me over their shoulder.

"Take her to the infirmary. Ollie will meet you there," Ric said. The person carrying me set me down on a bed.

"I have to get back. Keep her here and stay here yourself," he said.

"Andrea," Oliver said. "Open your eyes. I have to look at the wounds. I saw his concerned expression. "Ohh, god. You're infected. There's no one else here. I have to do it." his arms left my body for a few moments. "The one on your side is Wolfsbane. This is going to hurt. Brace yourself." I nodded.

He turned me on my side and I held one of his arms. He covered the wound with vervain powder. I shrieked as he touched the flame to my skin. The pain was impossible to express. I tried to push him away but he held me as steady as he could. He sat me up as I started coughing. I coughed up black goo and red blood.

"You're okay. The hardest part is over. The heather won't hurt as much." I laid back down. He brought over alcohol, long strips of cloth, a surgical needle, thread, and a bandage. He used the cloth and alcohol to clean the wound and he removed the bullet. He threaded the needle. "Close your eyes." I did and bit my lip as he closed the wound. I felt tears spill down my cheeks. He put on the bandage. "It's over, Andrea. You're okay," he breathed.

"Great." I swung my legs off the bed and marched back to the front hall, despite Oliver's protests. I grabbed my bow and arrows. I drove the elves back, helping my soldiers fall back into their formations. There was a part of me that was shocked that I could do this despite the injury I had just been treated for.

"Andrea! What are you doing?" Ric demanded.

"I'm doing my part. Let me. I'm all stitched up." I pulled Ric's sword from his belt and stabbed a stray elf trying to sneak up on him. "See, I'm helping," I boasted childishly. He took his sword back and swung it behind my back. "You don't have a 360-degree vision yet. Stay back, if you have to be here?"

"Fine," I said, shooting an elf with an arrow. It was another half hour before the remaining elves ran away. I sat down hard, dropping my bow. Eli knelt next to me.

"Are you okay?" I asked.

"I'm fine."

"And Celine and Alex."

"They're both fine. Ric ordered Celine to stay out of the fight with Freya. He would have locked you away too."

"I'm glad he didn't." I felt my strength waning.

"Can I help you get somewhere?"

"My room. I think I need to sleep. What time is it?"

"It's a little past midnight." He helped me to my feet and escorted me upstairs. I changed and laid face down on my bed and groaned. There was a knock on my door.

"Come in," I called as loudly as I could. Ric and Oliver came in.

"How are you? Are you feeling nauseous or lightheaded?" Ric asked.

"Not really. I'm okay."

"You have a very high resistance to wolfsbane."

"I guess so. How are you both doing?"

"We have been doing this for years. We're okay," Oliver said.

"I have to ask..." I began.

"Yeah?" Ric prompted.

"Why don't we use our wolf forms in battle?"

"The wolf helps our reflexes. Our battles are fought against creatures who use weapons. We can't fight with just our teeth. The wolf provides us with endurance, speed, and heightened senses. We can't depend on the wolf to fight for us. Haven't you noticed that for yourself?"

"I guess I didn't really pay much attention," I admitted.

"I heard you covering us with a sword last night. No normal person could have done that. Things slow down in our eyes.

"I'll pay attention next time," I said, the words sounding like mush.

"We'll let you sleep. Good night,"

I fell asleep as soon as the door closed.

16

I woke up to knocking on the door. "Come in," I said, getting up to brush my teeth. I came back to see Eli sitting on the couch.

"Hey," he said.

"Hey." I sat next to him. My leg touched his accidentally. It felt cold and unusually hard. "Eli your leg!" I exclaimed. He smiled at me.

"I have a metal leg. It's been there for years now."

"What?"

"From my hip down. There was too much wolfsbane in it."

"I never knew," I gawked.

"It's fine, Andrea."

"Can I see it?" I wondered.

He pulled the leg of his jeans up. I bent down, touching it gently. I followed it up to where his thigh would be. I blushed and looked up. My eyes widened as I found his face closer to mine than I thought it would be. He took my face in his hands gently and turned it so he could see me better. His eyes searched mine, looking for any sign that I was uncomfortable. He couldn't find any. My lips parted lightly in invitation. He leaned forward a few inches. My eyelids slid shut as he touched my lips with his, as lightly as a feather. I moved my arms to his neck, pulling my body closer to his.

"You should get ready for the day. Ric's expecting you," he said reluctantly moving his lips away from mine.

"Yeah," I agreed. I leaned forward for another kiss before he left my room and I went to shower. I dressed in a lacy black dress. It was sleeveless and reached my calves. It was regal yet daring. I tied up the front of the dress and went down.

"Your brother is in the war council miss," a guard said. I strode purposefully into the room.

"We've been waiting for you," Ric said.

"Sorry," I replied, blushing slightly. I sat in the empty chair next to Oliver.

"I'm ordering a recon mission today. Strictly recon only. Alex, you will lead the team. Take a troop with you. Andrea, Eli, and Oliver, you will join him."

"Where are we going?" I asked.

"To the Dokkalfar's lair. You need to gather all the intel you can without engaging. You'll be traveling with the sunlight and leave before dusk. Celine, send your best shooters."

"I could go myself," she suggested.

"I need you to stay here with me. The rest of you, take enough weapons and a first aid kit. You leave in twenty minutes. Andrea, can you move in that dress?"

"Yeah, Ric. I'm okay."

"Everyone go get your weapons. Celine, assign the troops."

I went to the armory and put blades on my legs. I hid my sword in my dress and took a gun. I adjusted my moonstone jewelry. I put a quiver of arrows over my shoulder and grabbed a bow. I went to the front room.

"Do you have any armor?" Oliver asked.

"I have some on," I assured. "How did you talk Ric into letting you come?"

"One of us had to come to take care of you. Ric wanted it to be him but he has duties here. As much as he wants to drop everything for you, he can't. So I told him I'd take you."

"And Celine?"

"Ric's not going to let her march into a Dokkalfar-infested lair." Celine came over with a group of armed soldiers.

"These soldiers will be coming with you. Be careful. Cover each other," she said as Eli and Alex arrived.

We got in the jeep. I was in the backseat with Oliver next to me. Eli drove as Alex swung himself into the passenger seat. We drove to the northern edges of New York. There were a few small hills hidden behind dense trees.

"The lair is somewhere in there. They won't be where sunlight can reach them. They have power over ice so it will get colder as we get closer to them," Eli said.

"Andrea, do you need a jacket?" Alex inquired gently.

"I'll be fine," I assured. We got out of the jeep. Alex was on point. I would walk behind him while Eli and Oliver covered my flanks. The battle troops followed us.

"Be very quiet," Alex warned. I unsheathed my sword and followed him. We walked for about a mile in the caves under the hill. We followed the coldness, letting it tell us which way to go. We figured the high commanders would be in the coldest part. We could barely see, even with our werewolf eyes. Ric and Alex were right to be concerned about my clothing choice. It wasn't hampering my movement but I was getting cold. I shivered lightly. Eli immediately took off the jacket he was wearing over a black turtleneck.

"Here, Andrea," he purred. I slipped my arms through it, grateful for the warmth.

"Thanks," I breathed back.

There was an opening in the rocks, through which we could see a group of Dokkalfar and the king. I was too scared to breathe. I covered my mouth, worried that a whimper might escape me, but fear shone in my eyes. These creatures took down my mother, with all her war training. I kicked myself mentally for being so scared and even more for showing it explicitly.

The elves were planning for war. There was a map of Brooklyn and the rest of the city. Alex, Eli, and Oliver were observing it and their conversation keenly. I couldn't deduce much from my fear. I did understand that they were talking about how to attack us. My breath was coming in short gasps. Someone touched my shoulder. I opened my mouth and shrieked in terror. The same hand covered my mouth, Oliver, while another rubbed my arm, Eli.

"It's just me," Oliver whispered into my ear. It was too late. The Dokkalfar had heard. The elves were grabbing their weapons.

"I'm sorry," I cried in fear. I hated that I was so scared. I was supposed to be Lilian's daughter, the alpha, Andrea Morgan.

"It's okay. Shh," Alex said, his voice a little too tense to be as gentle as he wanted to be. "Come on. We have to move quickly." He took point and Eli wrapped his arms tightly around me from behind, making sure my fear didn't stop me from moving. Oliver walked in front of me, holding my hand and pulling me along swiftly, making me move with them. I stumbled along, letting them move me. We were lucky to have the last rays of sun on our side. We climbed into the jeep quickly. I sat in the backseat, huddled in Oliver's arms.

"I'm sorry," I apologized again.

"It's okay to be scared, Andrea. You'll get better. It'll get easier to put your emotions aside when you need to. You just need to practice," Alex said.

"If I hadn't screamed, we would have had more time," I argued, my breathing still shallow.

"Andrea, it was almost dusk. I touched you to tell you that we had to leave," Oliver said, "You didn't sabotage anything." I nodded.

"Relax. We can all hear your heart racing," Alex said gently.

"I don't know how," I admitted, "I can't calm down." It was hard for me to admit my weakness.

"Listen to my heart," Oliver suggested gently, holding me against his chest. "Listen to my breathing... Close your eyes... Listen to my voice... You're safe. We'll be home soon. You'll be in your bed, in your room. There'll be guards there to protect you – Eli, drive to the apartment. Have Ric come there – I've got you, safe in my arms." I did as he suggested. I tried to control my breathing and calm down.

"Don't we have to brief Ric about the information we got?" Alex asked.

"He should be with Andrea now. It can wait until she is better."

"Sounds good," Alex agreed. Eli drove to my apartment while I kept concentrating on my breathing. Ric was waiting for us. He scanned me from head to toe picked me up and carried me up to my apartment. He set me on the couch and sat next to me.

"Is she hurt?" she demanded.

"No," I answered dryly.

"The Dokkalfar scared her," Oliver explained.

"Ohh, Andrea. I shouldn't have sent you out," Ric regretted.

"No! I want to be a part of things. I don't know why I was so scared."

"Hey, it's okay to be scared. You'll do better next time. It's fine," Ric assured.

"Ric, they're preparing for war," Oliver interrupted.

"What?" Ric shouted.

"They'll attack within the week by the looks of it," Alex provided.

"Are you sure?"

"Positive," Eli confirmed.

"Andrea, I'm so sorry that I can't stay with you. I have to go. Ollie, stay with her. I'll see you both tomorrow, after school," Ric said. He pulled off his T-shirt and ran out to take his wolf form. I was devastated that my brother couldn't stay with me tonight. I would have felt safer with Ric here.

"What do you want to do?" Oliver asked.

"I'm exhausted. I was going to go to bed." I decided not to let myself show fear.

"Before you do, can I see your waist?" he asked, awkwardly.

"My what?"

"I wanted to make sure your wound is healed."

"Ohh – Duh – sure. Give me a few minutes." I took a quick shower and put on my pajamas. I looked at my waist. It looked healed. I could barely see the wound, even against my pale skin. I went to the room Oliver was in.

"Can I see?" he asked. I moved my top aside in response. He touched the wound gently. I felt a twinge of unexpected pain. I didn't think there would be pain since I couldn't see the wound. He caught the pain shooting across my face.

"Sorry. You'll be fine in a few hours."

"What about you?" I asked responsibly.

He pulled his T-shirt off in one swift movement. I could clearly see where the bullets went through him. The skin was reddened. My fingers shivered as I reached to touch him. He took my hand and placed it on his chest. I traced the dots as gently as I could. I watched his face carefully for any sign that he was in pain.

"Am I hurting you?" I asked, unsure.

"I've waited so long to be with you, Andrea. Your touch does nothing but calm me down." I let my hand drop and he hugged me lightly. "Sleep well," he wished.

I woke up, ready to face the day with vigor. I dressed in a tight T-shirt and miniskirt. I pulled on knee-high boots and ponytailed my hair.

"Hey, Ollie. I'm going to pick Jack up. I'll see you later."

"Don't you want breakfast?" he asked, picking up my light mood. I smiled at him and grabbed a granola bar. He put a bottle of juice in my bag and took the wrapper from my hands. "Be careful, Andie."

"I will," I said, leaving. I drove to Jack's and he got in.

"Andie, what's going on? I haven't heard from you since the funeral."

"Well, on Friday night there was some gunfire. The Dokkalfar shot at my apartment. The next evening they attacked the facility. I helped drive them off. Yesterday, we went on a recon mission to their lair."

"What did you find out?" he asked eagerly.

"There's going to be a war within the week."

"A what?"

"A war. In New York City, Jack."

"Oh my god. What are you doing in school today with all that going on?"

"I have some research to do and I'm not just going to skip school."

"What research?"

"There are dark elves, right? There have to be light elves."

"That's a good point."

"I'm going to see what I can find out about them."

"I'll give you a hand." I spent an hour before lunch on the soccer field. I had traded my T-shirt for a jersey and laced up my sneakers. In the middle of practice, Jack opened a bottle of water and poured it over his face. It looked refreshing. I took a bottle, poured water into my palm, and splashed it on my face. After practice, I got dressed and went to the library. I pulled out a bunch of mythology books. I spent an hour poring over them.

After school, Jack and I went to my car. "I have to go to the facility. Do you want me to drop you off first?"

"Nah. I'll hang out there until you're done. Oh, wait. I don't have my ring on me."

"Here," I said, taking off my ring.

"Cool. Let's go." Oliver came up to the car as I was pulling out.

"Can you give me a ride to the facility?"

"Of course," I replied. "Get in." we drove to the facility and I went straight to Ric.

17

"Ric!" I called, interrupting the war council as I strode in purposefully. I was sure no one would question why I was here.

"Andrea? Come in," he invited despite that fact.

"I have to tell you something."

"Sure."

"The Ljosalfar, light elves. I spent the day researching them. If there are dark elves, there have to be light elves right?" I said, repeating my statement.

"Sit, Andrea. We've been talking about asking them for help."

"So, they do exist?"

"Of course they do. They're in an estate, or rather palace, in south New York."

"Okay..."

"Tomorrow, you and Ollie are going on a diplomatic mission to see them."

"Umm..." I hesitated.

"Don't worry. They're not scary. They're quite gentle beings. They fought with us in the last war. You'll present yourself as alpha – Ollie, join us," he said as Oliver peered into the room. "You and Andrea are going to the Ljosalfar tomorrow – you'll bring them a gift."

"What gift?" I asked as Oliver sat down.

"I'll get you something later. That's not important right now." I nodded in assent "You'll take a motorcycle. Dress in gentle, light colors. Andrea, Celine has an outfit for you. Ollie, a light T-shirt and pants. They won't hurt you but you still have to be alert. You'll ask them to help us. Orion and Hope will meet you there."

"Where's Celine?" I asked.

"She's feeding Freya. Go ahead."

I went to her room and knocked. "Come in," she called, "hey, Andrea."

"Hi." I smiled at her and cooed at her daughter, who was busy suckling away.

"You're here for your dress right?"

"Yeah, I am."

"Open the closet. It's on the first hanger on the right... This war, Ric's trying to get me to sit it out."

"It's because he knows that Freya needs her mother."

"I'm the best shooter and one of the best fighters he has."

"I think you should talk to him about it," I suggested. I took the dress. It was a pale golden piece. The top was a full-sleeved, fitted crop top and there was a skirt with a low waist that had four slits in it. "Some dress," I commented. The more clothes Celine chose for me, the more I could tell about her pre-pregnancy self. She must have been renowned for her beauty, her confidence, and her grace. Having Freya didn't take away from her beauty, but she was more focused on her daughter than on herself. This was pretty normal, but I still wanted to see the Celine that everyone looked up to and feared.

I took it to my room and hung it up. Just as I was about to sit down, I heard a deafening blast from the ground floor. I grabbed my sword and raced down.

It looked like a bomb had gone off. I whipped my head left and right. I clapped my palm over my mouth when I caught sight of Alex and Eli. Alex was lying motionless on the floor and Eli was hunched over himself. I ran to the boys and took Eli's face in my hands. I turned it to me.

"Are you okay?" I demanded, pressing my hand against his cheek. He nodded. I let go of him and shook Alex. "Alex!" I screamed. When he didn't respond, I pressed my fingers to his neck, checking for his pulse. I sighed in relief, feeling the blood racing through his veins. I turned back to Eli, turning his face so I could look at him. I grabbed him and pulled him into my arms. I kissed him hard for a moment. I was sure he could feel the relief in my lips when they pressed against his.

"I have to get Alex to the infirmary," Eli said, letting go of me reluctantly. I nodded and stood up. Eli stood up shakily. I had my arms half-extended in case he needed me to steady him.

"Are you sure you can take him to the infirmary on your own, Eli?" I asked.

"We can't spare anyone to help move the injured."

"Eli, you're hurt yourself."

"I can do it, Andrea," he insisted. I watched as he heaved Alex onto his shoulders and limped off. I went around helping others to their feet, making sure they were okay while assuring them that I wasn't hurt. It took Ric a while to find me.

"Andrea!"

"I'm fine. Really. I came down after the blast went off. We have to get them back for this."

"We will. Tomorrow, a troop will go blow holes into their lair. That will let sunlight in." I nodded and continued around the room. I helped some people to the infirmary. When I was there, I looked around for Eli and Alex.

"Have you seen Eli or Alex?" I asked a nurse. "They should be here."

"I'm sorry, Miss Andrea. I haven't seen them." That was odd. I crumpled my brow and went to find them.

I traced the routes from the ground floor to the infirmary. I found Eli on the ground with Alex on top of him. Eli's legs must have given way. I rushed over to the boys and dropped to my knees next to them. I managed to roll Alex off of Eli's body. I was shocked to feel his body temperature. It was higher than normal. "Eli," I called, hoping he would regain consciousness. He told me that he wasn't hurt. I was devastated that he hadn't been honest with me.

I looked around for anyone I could call over for help. Luckily, two soldiers passed by me just then. They approached me and I helped them heave the boys over their shoulders. I followed them to the infirmary where they set them on the beds. A few nurses came over to check them out. Ric walked in as the nurse finished.

"What's wrong with the boys?" he demanded.

"Alex was merely knocked unconscious. Eli might have a little concussion, sir," she answered brusquely. I sat in between both boys as I waited for them to wake up. Celine wandered in as Alex opened his eyes.

"Hey..." I greeted brightly.

"Hey, Andrea," he groaned.

"How do you feel?" I demanded, brushing his hair back.

"I'm just tired," he admitted. I smiled at him.

"Do you want to go up to your bed?" Celine inquired gently. She was so maternal.

"Yes, mom," Alex accepted, teasing her. Celine stood up and helped Alex to his feet. He put one arm around her as she led him out of the infirmary. A man came to summon Ric.

"Andrea, tell me if Eli doesn't wake up," he instructed before leaving. I nodded and sat next to Eli's head. I kissed his forehead. His eyes fluttered open. I sighed in relief.

"My head hurts," he groaned.

"Ohh, Eli, it will be okay. You're going to be fine. Will you let me take you up to your room so you can get some sleep?" He nodded and grimaced at the discomfort the movement caused. I had to move him because there were other injuries that needed to be treated. There weren't a lot of beds in the infirmary.

I gently pulled him to his feet and I led him upstairs. I walked into his room and helped him into bed. He groaned and closed my eyes. "I'll be back soon, Eli. Call me if you need me," I ordered, making sure he could reach his phone.

I found Ric, Celine, and Oliver in the war council.

"Eli's awake," I informed. A collective sigh ran around the room.

"Any casualties?" Celine asked me.

"Not that I know of."

"One casualty," Ric corrected.

"Who?" Celine asked.

"The elder, Annabelle. Ollie, Andrea, go to bed. You have an important job tomorrow."

I went into Eli's room. I lay next to him, careful not to jostle him. I felt him cuddle up against my shoulder. His hair tickled my neck. "I love you," I whispered into his ears.

I woke up early and slipped out of Eli's room. I took a shower and dressed in a pair of shorts and armor. I pulled on the skirt and top. The sleeves were tight to my elbows and then were loosely flared. The skirt was showy but covered my shorts. I strapped on a thigh holster and stuck a gun in it. I hid my sword in the folds of my skirt. I put on golden, high-heeled sandals and brushed my hair. I hung on some jewelry. To finish off, I put on a hooded black cloak for some coverage on the road. I stuffed a T-shirt into a backpack and went downstairs.

"Andrea, why are you wearing a cloak?" Ric asked.

"I'm traveling by motorcycle. I need some cover."

"That sounds reasonable. Here, this box contains an eternal flame. Present it to the king. Introduce yourself as the alpha. Be very polite and careful when you speak to him." I put the box in my bag and Oliver came in.

"The bike's up front. Are you ready?" he asked.

"Let's do it," I replied. Ric helped me across the swamp and onto the bike. I pulled up my hood and put my hands on Oliver's shoulders.

"Good luck and be careful," Ric wished. "Andrea, hold on tight."

"Make sure Eli's okay," I requested.

He nodded and Oliver revved the engine. He drove to the city to the outskirts. There was a single windy road that we went down. We stopped in front of a beautiful white castle with a drawbridge. I got off the bike and so did Oliver. Orion and Hope ran up to us.

"Hey," I greeted offhandedly.

"State your purpose," a guard ordered.

"The alpha of the Eclipse pack of Brooklyn, Andrea, here to visit the king of the Lsojalfar," Oliver announced. The drawbridge opened and I let my hood fall. Oliver formally offered me his arm. I took it gratefully, worried I would trip in my outrageous footwear. Our wolves walked in front of us and I clutched Oliver's arm tightly. A couple of handmaidens approached us as we crossed the threshold.

"Your cloak," they offered. I slipped it off, revealing my dress. I took my brother's arm again and they led us to what looked like the throne room. I knelt gracefully in front of who I assumed to be the king and Oliver followed my lead.

"The alpha of the Eclipse pack, Andrea," someone announced.

"Rise, alpha," the king commanded. I stood while Oliver remained kneeling next to me.

"My pack sends their respect, Your Majesty," I said, curtsying. He nodded in acknowledgment. Oliver passed me the box. "I have a gift for his majesty. I present an eternal flame." I placed it on a tray and the attendant gave it to the king. He examined it keenly.

"Join me for lunch in one hour," he said simply.

"Thank you, your majesty," I agreed. The king left the chamber and Oliver stood up.

"That was easy," he commented, scratching Hope.

"It's not over yet," I reminded.

"That dress..." he began.

"What, is it sticking up somewhere?" I asked, nervously smoothening the skirt.

"No! I was going to ask you if it was comfortable."

"Ohh. Yeah, it's alright, Ollie."

"What do you want to do?"

"Find somewhere to sit and wait. I don't want to do a lot of walking." We went to sit on a bench in an indoor garden.

A guard approached us a while later. "His Majesty invited you to join him in the dining room." Oliver and I went with the guard and were seated across from the king.

"Lady Andrea, we take great pleasure in having you here with us."

"The pleasure is mine, Your Majesty. May I introduce my brother, Oliver?"

The king nodded at Oliver. "Why have you traveled all this way? I know you – shall we say – base is far from my palace."

"Your Majesty, I believe you are aware that the Dokkalfar have been active recently. They have attacked us three times in the past two days. They are preparing for war to begin by the end of the week."

"We have noticed suspicious Dokkalfar activity, Lady Andrea. What do you propose?"

"An alliance, Your Majesty. My pack needs all the help it can get."

"Are you Lilian's daughter?" he asked abruptly.

"I am," I confirmed. "You knew my mother?"

"Yes. I was a prince during the last war. I commanded my army at your mother's side. She was a powerful and beautiful woman and an extraordinary commander."

"As my mother's only daughter, I sincerely request your assistance, Your Majesty."

"Will your commanders be available to meet with mine?" he demanded.

"Yes. My elder brother, Ric, is one of our chief commanders. He will meet with yours at any time you please."

"Very well. Some of my commanders will accompany you to your base today. Please, eat now."

After lunch, the king introduced us to his commanders. They followed us home on horses. Ric was waiting with guards at the swamp. A bridge had been constructed to cross over. It had obviously been built today, but it looked steady.

"Please, follow Ric and Oliver to our war council. I'll join you shortly," I said as the commanders dismounted. I crossed the bridge and Ric discreetly signaled a guard to follow me. I went to my room and he waited outside. I changed into black jeans and a tank top. I stuck blades in my boots and went to the war council. Ric and the commanders had a long conversation and the elves talked about war strategy. I had trouble following the conversation but acted like I understood. I could tell that Ric was making sure no one questioned me. I sat back and let him handle everything, contributing only what was necessary. A few hours later, Ric offered to take them on a tour of the facility. I excused myself and went upstairs.

I opened the door of Eli's room, eager to check on him. He was sitting up in bed.

"Hey," he invited.

"How are you feeling?" I asked.

"I feel better, Andrea."

"Ric's giving a few Ljosalfar commanders a tour. We should go help him."

He smiled at me. "Come here for a minute,"

I went to him and he had me sit on his lap. One of his arms went around me and the other rested on my cheek. He kissed me gently and brushed my hair back. The kiss was perfect, so chaste.

"You're so beautiful," he whispered. I felt heat rise to my cheeks. He helped me to my feet and we went down. We found Ric in the hall of alphas. I went to him and took his arm. I smiled cordially at the commanders. The tour went on for another hour. I stayed at Ric's side throughout it. Oliver was on guard, his eyes always sweeping our surroundings, they often lingered on me for longer than necessary.

After the tour, we went to dinner. I took the alpha's place at the head of the table. Ric tucked my chair in and sat on my right. Oliver was on my left. By the time the commanders left, I felt like we had won them over. I was exhausted. I had school tomorrow and needed sleep.

"I want to go home," I complained like a child.

"Andrea, why don't you sleep here tonight?" Ric suggested. I shrugged and went up to my room. I showered and lay on the bed. My hair was damp but I didn't have the energy to dry it. I laid face down on the bed. There was a knock on my door.

"Mmm..." I invited. I saw Eli come in.

"Are you okay?" he asked. I nodded. He sat next to me with something in his hands. He took my hair and rubbed his hands through it. He had a towel and was drying my hair.

"Thanks," I whispered.

"Can I get you anything else?"

"No," I mumbled, my words sounding like nonsense.

"I'll see you in the morning." I felt him get up.

"Eli," I whispered.

"Yeah?"

"Stay," I breathed, losing consciousness.

18

I woke up, ready to take on the world. I stretched and hopped into the shower. I dressed in bell-bottom pants, a pink tank top, and a jacket. I put on sneakers and stuck a blade to my calf. I ponytailed my hair and went down with my bag. I grabbed a couple pieces of toast for breakfast. Oliver came up to me in a few minutes.

"Hey, little sis. Ready to go?"

"We're the same age, Ollie," I protested.

"We'll talk about it later. Come on," he diverted.

We drove to school in my car. Liam drove up just as we got out of the car. His jaw dropped seeing us together.

"No way. Impossible. Are you two together? Is that why you're avoiding me, Morgan?" Liam demanded.

"Excuse me, your attitude is why I'm avoiding you."

"Andrea, hold on," Oliver intervened. "Liam, you've got it all wrong."

Jack came up to us. "Andie, what's going on?"

"Uhh, Russell, not you too. West, what do I have wrong?"

"Liam, I told you I was adopted. My guardian is my old foster brother, Ric. The same guy who's Andrea's stepbrother."

"So what? I suppose that's the story she fed you when you were making out."

I was about to punch his jaw when Oliver did it himself. "I swear, if you ever say another word against my sister, you'll wish you'd never laid eyes on her. Stay away from her. Andrea come on." Oliver grabbed my arm tightly and pulled me away from Liam. Jack followed us to the gym.

"Ollie, calm down," I said, "I thought you liked Liam."

"Not if he's insulting someone I care about."

"Look, thank you for being chivalrous, but I can take care of myself. Now, you have to find Liam and try to apologize. He's your best friend."

"And you're my sister."

"Ollie, go ahead. I'll see you later." He hugged me and left quietly.

"What was all that?" Jack asked.

"Liam saw me and Oliver together and he kind of erupted. He thought we were dating and that Oliver betrayed him."

"Ohh,"

"We should get to class." On the way, I ran into the student body president.

"Hey, Andrea."

"Hey man, what's up?"

"How are the plans for this week's dance going?" that caught me off guard. I totally forgot about the dance. I had to pick a theme.

"Great," I fibbed. "I'm calling a meeting at lunch today to tell everyone about the theme. Can you spread the word?"

"Sure," he left and Jack gaped at me.

"How did you have time to think of the dance with everything that's going on?"

"I didn't. I'll come up with something."

"Good luck with that," We went to class and I spent the morning racking my brain. I went to the bleachers at lunch to wait for the rest of the dance committee and student council to show up. I cleared my throat a few minutes later.

"Hey, can you all hear me? Great. The theme of this week's dance is supernatural. Like werewolves, vampires, witches, monsters, elves, whatever other mythological creatures there are. It will be in the gym, as usual. I want the decorations to be dark. I want to give off a cheesy horror flick vibe. We'll get flyers today. The timings will be as usual, from 6-11." I finished up quickly and excused myself to get to soccer practice. I changed into my jersey and went to the field.

"Sorry, coach. I had a committee meeting."

"Get in there." After practice, I approached our coach. "What is it, Morgan?"

"Coach, I don't know if I can stay on the team."

"Why not?"

"I'm cheer captain and head of the dance committee. There's also stuff I have to deal with at home."

"You're a natural kid, I need you. I don't care if you show up to practice or not, but you have to play. You're the best player I've seen."

"You do know that I have no idea how to really play, right? I can only score."

"You can score every single time. Look, I'll take the boys out of cheer if that makes things easier. I'm not letting you quit."

I nodded reluctantly. Liam and Oliver weren't at practice and I hadn't seen them in class all day.

"Jack, I need a favor."

"Yeah. Sure."

"Go to the locker room and get me Oliver's shirt."

"What? Never mind, sure." He left and I waited in the parking lot. He came back with a T-shirt balled up in his hands. He threw it to me and I held it to my nose, memorizing Oliver's scent so I could track him. I gave Jack the shirt and inhaled deeply, focused on what I could smell. I found his scent and tracked it. It took me a few tries to get it right. Jack and I went to the trees behind the school. I walked into the trees and my jaw dropped.

I saw Oliver's body lying facedown on the ground. His body was completely bare. I pulled off my jacket, exposing myself to the cool breeze, and threw the jacket over Oliver's body.

"Ollie," I whispered, touching him. I turned him on his back and gasped again. His chest and face were covered in what looked like punch marks. "Jack, his clothes have to be around here somewhere."

"Sure," he agreed and left. With trembling fingers, I touched Oliver's neck, looking for a pulse. I sighed in relief as I felt blood rushing under my fingers. I brushed his hair back. He woke with a start.

"Ollie," I breathed.

"Give me my clothes," he said to Jack. Jack did and Oliver stood up, not meeting my eyes. I waited until he was done.

"Are you okay?" I asked.

"Werewolf healing. I'll be okay in an hour. I'll see you later, Andrea."

"Are you going home?"

"You're forgetting that I don't have a home. I don't have anyone to stand up for me." I pulled out my keys and pressed them into his hands. I placed my palm on his cheek and he winced.

"You have me," I promised. He looked at me for a second and hugged me. I felt him tremble a little. "Take my car too. Jack will drop me off." He nodded and walked away. I felt a cold breeze on my waist. Oliver had taken my jacket with him.

"Let's get inside," I suggested. Jack drove me home later.

"Do you want me to come with you, Andie?"

"Thanks, Jack. I'll be okay though." I went up and threw my bag on the couch. I knocked on Oliver's room and went in. he wasn't in bed. I noticed that the bathroom door was cracked open. I sat on the bed to wait for him. An hour passed and he still hadn't come out. I took a towel and cracked open the door.

He was sitting in the tub, fully dressed, with the shower on. I reached in to shut off the water and sat on the edge of the tub. I wrapped the towel around him and he leaned into me. His head rested on my lap. I rubbed his shoulders reassuringly. I understood why he left the shower on. I saw tears leaking out of his eyes, undisguised, now that I had turned off the shower. I pretended not to notice and continued to soothe him.

"Do you want to tell me about it?" I asked a while later. He nodded once. "Get dressed, Ollie. I'll be right back." He nodded again and moved his head. I kissed his head before I went to my room and changed. I threw my wet clothes in the hamper. I went back to his room. He was curled up on his bed. I sat next to him and he moved his head to my lap.

"What happened?" I asked gently.

"I went to talk to him like you said... and we talked... but it felt strange... He took me out back before soccer practice and..." he stammered between tears, hesitating.

"It's me, Ollie, I won't judge."

"He didn't believe me when I told him that nothing was going on between us... He started attacking me... He wants you, Andrea. He'll do anything he wants to get you. He's wicked and cruel and the only thing he wants is my sister," he choked out.

"Nothing could draw me to him." We stayed that way for a few minutes. I wiped the tears off his face gently. "Hey, can I ask you something?"

"Sure."

"Why have I never heard of you with a girl?"

"Umm, I've never really had a girlfriend."

"Why not?"

"She would ask about my family and there's nothing I could have told her."

"Okay, but if you could, who would you want to date?"

"Your friend Allison," he admitted.

"Really?"

"Yeah, but I'm sure she would never go out with me."

"You're Oliver West, one of the most popular guys in school."

"It would mean telling people about us, that we are family."

"It's fine. Go for it."

"Are you sure?"

"Positive." My phone rang, startling us. "Hey, Ric."

"Are you and Ollie at home?"

"Yeah, we are."

"Get to the facility. We need you both here for training and war council."

"What is it?" Oliver asked as I hung up.

"Ric wants us at the facility. Come on... if you're okay."

"I'm fine, go get changed."

"I'm ready to go," I said, standing up. I took my phone and went to my car. Oliver got in the passenger seat. "Ollie, are you really okay or are you just saying that so I quit bothering you? You know, we could go to the cops if you want."

"We don't have any proof."

"You're proof."

"Give me your hand." I did and he put it on his chest, under his shirt. He was all healed. "Werewolf healing."

"I forgot."

"I'll be okay."

"Look, you have to ask Allison to the dance."

"With the war, I don't know if we can even go."

"Just ask her." He ruffled my hair and smiled. I decided to leave him alone with his thoughts. We found Ric in the war council.

"The battle will be on Saturday at dusk. Our allies will be here that morning. Excuse me please, I need to speak with my siblings," Ric concluded. The room emptied quickly. "How are you both?"

"We had an interesting day," Oliver conceded.

"Why did you need us?" I asked.

"Today and tomorrow, we're training the wolves. I thought you'd like to be here."

"Sure. Ollie and I will be at school late on Friday. We have a dance and Ollie's going to have a real date."

"Well, you can't miss that. Have fun. Now, go out to the wolf arena. I'll try to meet you there later." Oliver led me to the arena. There were so many wolves there, it scared me. I stopped at the entrance. Oliver put his arm around me.

"It's okay. Nothing here will hurt here, Andrea." I nodded and regained my composure. I strode into the room. I couldn't do much to help, but I sat there, watching. Celine found me a few hours later. She had a stack of index cards in her hands.

"Andrea, Ric had me make these for you. They are about our war strategies and formations. You're going to be our chief commander."

"That's Ric's job."

"He's alpha as long as you need him to, but you have to present yourself as one. He'll help you, but you need to know these."

"I have no idea how I'm going to learn all these."

"You'll be great. You're a natural at being a werewolf. You were born to do this."

"Thanks. Can I borrow the most wolf-ish dress you have?"

"Sure. Why though?"

"School dance on Friday. It's supernatural-themed."

"Come on up," she laughed.

I followed her up to her room and she pulled some dresses from her closet. One was short, thigh length, backless, and fitted with a deep neck. Another was full and long. It was also V-necked and backless, it would be fitted until my thighs and then flared behind me, open in the front. They were both black and heavy and were opaque and transparent at the same time.

"I'll take the long one," I said.

"It's yours," she agreed. "Here, this jewelry goes with it."

"Thanks, Celine, you're the best."

There was a knock on the door. Oliver stuck his head through the doorway.

"Andrea, are you ready to go home?"

"Yeah." Celine put the dress in a bag and handed it to me. Ric was at the foot of the stairs.

"I'm sorry. I can't come home with you guys tonight or for the next few days. I promise I'll be more responsible and attentive once things cool down." He hugged us and we went to the car. I drove home and hung up my dress.

"Andrea, I'm going to bed. I'll see you tomorrow."

"Good night," I replied. Before I fell asleep, I looked at the box of accessories Celine gave me. They looked like they were made of obsidian. They were elaborate and beautiful.

19

I bolted up in the middle of the night to terrifying, piercing shrieks. I tumbled out of bed and rushed into Oliver's room, brandishing my sword. He was thrashing around wildly. I thought he was having a fit. Tears streaked down his cheeks freely. My sword clattered to the ground and I launched myself at him. I grabbed his arms first, holding them against his chest. It took both my hands to restrain his. I used my legs to pin him on the bed. I positioned myself so that his head was resting on my chest so I could comfort him when he woke up while still restraining him. My legs were on his side, one of them over his.

"Hey, hey, Ollie, it's Andie. Look at me. You're home, Ollie. Open your eyes." He thrashed for a few more minutes, trying to tear his hands away from mine. I was worried he would hurt himself if I let him go. He met my eyes moments after he settled. I let go of his legs and sighed.

"Andie?" he asked, his eyes still wild.

"I'm here. What happened?"

"I had a nightmare," he stated, wiping his nose on the sleeve of his shirt. "I used to have them at the orphanage too. I'd scream myself awake. The only difference is that I'd be all alone when I woke up."

"You have me now, Ollie. It was just a dream. You're okay. Do you want to talk about it?"

"Not really..." he admitted.

"That's alright, Ollie. I'm here if you want to talk. Why don't we talk about something else?"

"Okay... Who are you going to the dance with?"

"I don't usually take anyone, Ollie. I stick to the planning. Jack and I just hang out together. I was going to invite Eli. I don't know if he'd come though."

"He'll be there. If you ask him, he'll come."

"Fine, I will. Are you ready to go back to sleep?"

"I'll try."

"Yell for me if you need me, Ollie. I'll see you in the morning." I tucked my brother in and went back to my room. I called Eli.

"Andrea, it's past midnight. Are you okay?"

"Yeah. Umm..."

"What is it?"

"There's a school dance on Friday."

"Ohh."

"I mean, if you can spare the evening. It's okay. I know you and Ric have your duties at the facility," I rambled.

"Andrea, hold on. I'd be happy to join you."

"Really?"

"Of course."

"Great. It's supernatural-themed. I'm going as a werewolf alpha."

"You are an alpha," he said in mock innocence.

"You know what I mean."

"Yeah. I'll see you on Friday evening and probably before that too."

"Sure, good night." I hung up and smiled.

I spent the next two days preparing for the dance. Oliver came up to our lunch table the day after he had his nightmare.

"Hey," we all said, the way we'd greet anyone else.

"Hey, ladies. Allison?"

"Yeah?"

"Is anyone taking you to the dance?"

"No. Wait, are you asking me, Oliver? I thought you were dating Andrea."

"I am asking you. Andrea is my adoptive sister. Her older brother is my guardian."

"Wait hold on. Andrea, your brother?"

"Yeah. Apparently, my mom fostered him when he was little. Now back to the question."

"Sure, Oliver. I'd love to go with you. Should I meet you here?" she asked, hoping he'd pick her up.

"Pick her up," I breathed, knowing his wolf ears would hear me.

"I'll pick you up around 5:30."

"Great," she agreed. He turned away after squeezing my shoulder gently. "Who are you going with then, Andrea?"

"I'm going with my older brother's friend. Eli. The theme is supernatural. I'm dressing up as a fierce werewolf alpha. What about you girls?"

"I'm going as a vampire queen," Alisson said.

"She-devil," Katie provided.

"An elf," Sophia informed.

"Andrea, what about your friend Jack," Katie asked innocently.

"Ohh no! You are not going anywhere near him. Not after that stunt you pulled. He's not bringing a date."

Before the dance, I took a relaxing bubble bath. I pulled on a bathrobe as Oliver knocked on the door. He was dressed as a vampire, to complement Allison. I opened the door for him. He was in a tuxedo and had made his face pale. He painted some blood on his chin. I took my red lipstick and outlined his lips.

"You look great, Ollie. Have fun. My keys are on the table."

"How will you get there?"

"Eli will be here soon. I'll see you there." He left and I put on my dress. I did my makeup to highlight the streak in my hair. I styled my hair high and put on my jewelry. I stepped into my heels and looked into the mirror. I looked perfect. For the finishing touch, I exposed my fangs and claws. I made sure my birthmark was visible.

The door of my apartment opened and closed.

"Andrea," Eli called.

"One second!" I replied. I grabbed my phone and stuffed it into my clutch. I adjusted the translucent train and went to the living room. Eli was in a simple tuxedo with a few claw marks on it.

"Hey," I said shyly.

"You look beautiful. Where did you get this dress?"

"It's Celine's," I admitted.

"It suits you. Are you ready to go?" I took his arm and he led me to a car. He helped me in and drove me to school.

"Where's Ollie?" he asked suddenly.

"He had to pick up his date. He should be at the dance." Eli offered me his arm as I got out of the car.

"Don't be formal, Eli," I said. He put his arm over my shoulders in an attempt to be casual. "Much better," I teased.

"What's with the claws?" he whispered.

"That's not all I have," I said, pulling my lips back carefully. "I'm a werewolf alpha, remember."

"Of course." We walked into the gym. I smiled to myself, admiring my handwork.

"You arranged all this?" he asked.

"I did."

"It's beautiful. Will you dance with me?"

"Of course,"

He led me out. "You do know how to dance right?" he asked.

"Do you" I countered.

"I've seen people dancing before," he compromised.

"Here," I took his hand and placed it on my waist. I wound the other around my back. I put one of my hands on his shoulder and the other around his neck. I started revolving and he let me lead.

"Not so hard," he commented.

After the song, Allison waved us over.

"Hey," I greeted.

"Dude, you look amazing," Allison complimented. "You look like you were born to be a werewolf." I smiled at her comment.

"Thanks, Allison. You look beautiful too." Her vampire costume was simple, a black knee-length dress and red lipstick."

"You can be honest, Andrea. I know I look simple. I wasn't sure exactly how to pull it off," she admitted.

"You could have chosen dramatic makeup," I provided.

Liam walked in a while later. He hadn't been in school for the past couple of days. I was dancing with Eli and he marched up to me.

"Explain, Morgan," he growled.

"I don't have anything to say," I replied, trying to remain calm.

"Who's your date?" he demanded.

"I'm Eli," Eli intervened.

"Eli, hold on. Liam, what do you want?"

"I wanted to see you. Damn, it was worth it. You look smoking hot, Morgan. How does your dress even stay up?"

"Andrea," Eli began. I held up a finger, telling him to wait. I wanted to deal with him myself.

"Don't you have anything else to say?" I demanded.

"Hmm," He grabbed me, putting one palm on my bare back and the other held my chin. I shivered at his touch. I was horrified at the turn this was taking. Before anyone could react, he kissed my lips hard and moved down my neck. He gripped my shoulders and kissed my chest. Everyone around me was frozen in shock.

"Get off me," I growled, snarls building in my throat.

"Get off her," Eli and Oliver snarled at the same time. I freed myself from his grip and Allison pulled me back. A group had gathered around us.

"What's going on?" the coach asked. He was chaperoning tonight.

"Liam was about to hurt Andrea," Allison exclaimed indignantly.

"Liam, get over here. Ms. Morgan, are you alright?" I nodded as Eli wrapped his arms protectively around me. "Liam, what were you thinking?"

"She looked super-hot and I wanted her. I've been asking her out but she won't come."

"You've earned yourself a session with the school counselor and lost your position as captain. Now, get out of here!" coach ordered.

Liam shot a look of contempt at the coach, winked at Oliver, and left.

"Thanks, coach," Oliver said.

"West, are you here with Morgan? Take her home."

"No, I'm here with Allison."

"Ms. Morgan, are you sure you're okay?"

"Just shaken up. Thanks, coach."

"Maybe you should get yourself home," he suggested.

I nodded and leaned into Eli. The coach left.

"Ollie, I'm taking her home. Meet us at my place," Eli said, referring to the facility.

"Oliver, you should go too. I'll catch a ride home," Allison said.

"No Allison, he should make sure you get home safely." Oliver gave me a gentle hug and Eli led me out. He took off his tuxedo and put it around my shoulders.

"Thanks, Eli," I said, in the car.

He drove to the facility and helped me over the bridge. "Go get changed and then see Ric," he suggested.

I went up to my room and locked the door. I took a hot bath and washed all the makeup off my face. I dressed in a tank top and shorts. Some of the Ljosalfar commanders were here. The rest would arrive in the morning. There was a knock on the door and I went to open it.

"Hey, Ollie. Did you get Allison home?"

"Yeah." He sat on the bed next to me. His lips were still bright red. I used the heel of my palm to wipe it off. "Ric's looking for you."

"I should go see what he needs," I agreed.

"It's for dinner with the Ljosalfar," he provided.

"Ohh. I don't think this is appropriate attire," I groaned. I didn't want to change clothes. Oliver laughed as I pulled a floor-length skirt out of my closet. I slipped into it and tied my hair up. He put an arm around me as we went down to Ric.

He was in the dining hall with the elders and some of our commanders. I sat next to Ric and tried to keep up with the conversation. I didn't know what the morning would bring, but I knew I had to be brave.

Eli walked me up to my room after dinner. "Will you stay," I asked, feeling pathetic.

"Of course." I hung up my skirt and he took off his T-shirt. "I hope this doesn't make you uncomfortable," he said.

"I'm okay," I assured. He laid on the bed and I cuddled close to him. I sighed as his strong fingers touched my back. I rested my head on his chest and let his breath lull me to sleep.

I woke up to an empty bed in the morning. I assumed Eli went to prepare for the war. I showered and dressed in skinny jeans and armor like Celine showed me. I ponytailed my hair and grabbed my sword. I pulled on my boots and marched downstairs.

"Hey, Andie," Oliver greeted. He was the first to see me.

"Hey, Ollie." He threw me a granola bar that I scarfed down. We walked into the war council together. Things were already in full swing there. Ric was in full body armor and the Ljosalfar king was at the table. I bowed to him and Ric directed me to the head of the table.

"I hope you're well, Your Majesty. Thanks again for assisting us."

"The Dokkalfar are our traditional enemies Lady Andrea." The preparation continued until noon. After that, I went with Alex to inspect the troops. They were dispatched to take their places around the city.

20

It was time for me to get ready too. I went to my room and saw the alpha's war regalia on my bed. First, I changed into black denim shorts that would allow free movement. The combat boots were knee-high. I pulled them on and secured my breastplate. It was a perfect fit. I stuck my sword in my belt and put on the weapon holsters. I took my helmet and went to the armory. Celine and Alex were handing out weapons. I was handed knives, guns, my bow, and a quiver full of arrows. I armed myself and went to find Eli. He was looking at screens in his office, the control room.

"Andrea, are you ready?"

"As ready as I'll ever be," I admitted.

"You'll do great, he assured me, placing his arm on my waist. He pulled me closer and tilted my chin up. He kissed me gently and let go.

I went to Oliver next. "Andie, you look just like your mother," he commented. "I've seen pictures of her in her war regalia."

"Thanks, Ollie. I hope I can live up to her standards."

"You're Andrea Morgan. You can do anything." I hugged him, careful not to him, and went to the front room.

"Andrea, do you want to ride in the jeep or motorcycle? The elves will be on horseback," Ric asked.

"What do you think?"

"I can have Ollie drive you either way. I'd prefer you were in a jeep with Orion."

"What about you?"

"I'm leaving now. I'll be on the bridge with the king. Follow as soon as you can."

"How are you getting there?"

"I'm taking Celine on a motorcycle."

"I'll see you there, brother." He kissed my forehead and marched out. Someone brought me a heavy black cloak. The elves I saw around the facility were in gleaming silver armor, moving around purposefully. I put on my cloak and waited for Oliver. Orion reached me first. I hadn't seen him in a while.

"Hey boy," I greeted. He playfully butted my leg with his nose. Oliver came over in heavy battle armor. He took my hand and led me out. He helped me into the passenger seat and got in himself. I pulled up my hood and fiddled with my bow as Oliver drove. We left the jeep at the end of the tree line and Oliver walked me to the Ljosalfar king and Ric.

"Lady Andrea," the king greeted.

"Your Majesty, my thanks again for your assistance."

"Alpha, you should go check on your troops," Ric suggested as I lowered my hood. I knew he was trying to send me back to safety. I wasn't having that.

"I am sure you positioned them well, Ric. I'd rather stay on point." I said, shouldering my bow and clutching the hilt of my sword in my belt. I waited with Ric and the king with our troops behind us. Looking back at it, the anticipatory waiting was harder than the actual battle.

When it began, it was quick and immediate. The Dokkalfar arrived with the twilight. We heard battle cries after the last rays of sunlight had disappeared.

"Team Theta!" I called clearly as Ric went to take his place in the army. He told me that the wolves would cover me. I protested that I could cover my own territory but he pretended not to hear me. The first battalion charged forth with Ric in the lead. They ran past me and charged into battle.

I pulled out my sword, ready to jump into battle. "Team Omega!" I called next. I saw Oliver barrel past me with the second battalion, which he commanded. I barely had a second to pray for him before I had to call on Eli. "Team Sirius!" I ordered.

A few minutes later, "Team Lucifer! Team Andromeda!" I called clearly, referring to Alex and Celine's battalions. The Ljosalfar king retreated behind his personal guard. I, however, marched into battle with Orion by my side. I drew my blades and started hacking away.

A while later, I felt tears pool in my eyes. I had just glanced around the battlefield and saw Celine being stabbed in the back by a deadly sword. She fell and Ric gave an anguished cry. I watched him sprint to take down Celine's attacker. He wasn't paying attention to anything else and got shot. I clapped my palm over my mouth in horror.

"Andrea! Behind you!" Alex shouted. I hadn't noticed some elves surrounding me. I stabbed one in the heart and pressed a hidden button that set the blade on fire – the Dokkalfar's weakness. The Dokkalfar disintegrated. I couldn't use my bow in close quarters. I used my flaming sword to cut another one in half. A couple of soldiers took down the other two elves. I whipped my head around, searching. I found Alex single-handedly taking on a troop of Dokkalfar. I drew my bow and strung an arrow. I hit the button the shaft that set the tip on fire. I shot the heart of the elf closest to Alex as Eli rushed to help him. He couldn't help. They both were defeated and collapsed. They had been stabbed. I screamed as I saw my friends lying motionless. I screamed so loud I thought I saw some lights flicker in buildings miles away.

My heart skipped a beat and picked up in double time. Our most skilled warriors were dropping like flies. I frantically scanned the field for Oliver. He was lying unconscious in the heart of the battle, as a troop of Dokkalfar closed in on him. I ordered a group of my wolves to flank me. I pulled out my knives and hacked my way through some Dokkalfar to Oliver. The wolves covered me as I dropped next to him. Orion held my bow in his jaw. I felt for a pulse in Oliver's neck and then pulled him back, out of the line of fire.

My breath came in short gasps. The entire army was looking to me for instruction. Ric couldn't help me. Neither could Eli or Alex or Oliver or Celine, sweet Celine who had a beautiful baby waiting for her at home. I couldn't let Freya lose her mom. But I wasn't ready for this.

Ric promised me he would help me as long as I needed it, but now I was all alone in the middle of a war. I wasn't an Alpha. I wanted to cower behind the Ljosalfar guard and let them do all the work. I was just a seventeen-year-old girl from Brooklyn. I wasn't a warrior or a leader. I had no idea what I was doing here.

I was terrified, quaking in my boots. Two months ago I was a normal teenager, a cheerleader, a high schooler. Now, I had so much to live up to. My mother Lilian, her bravery and courage. My father Nicolas, his honesty and determination. My brother Ric, his leadership and fearlessness. I felt the expectations weighing me down, pushing me into the asphalt. My head spun dizzily and I felt sweat pool on my palms. I focused on evening my breathing. I felt hundreds of eyes on me and something clicked. I steeled myself and exhaled.

"Beta Formation! Fall back!" I commanded. I watched my pack organize themselves instantly. They retreated, but stopped in front of me, their loyalty towards me unwavering. I had to repay them.

"Get back!" I called. "Stay behind me." My orders were followed instantly. I saw my friends – my family – being taken behind the lines, to safety. I pulled out my sword and bared my fangs. I snarled ferociously, reacting to the growls around me.

"On my position, for my mother! Lilian. For the Eclipse pack! Charge!" I ordered.

"For Lilian!" the army echoed and followed me. My vision tunneled, focusing on each Dokkalfar in turn. I used my years of cheerleading practice and vaulted behind the front line of the Dokkalfar. The wolf in me let me land steadily on my feet, sword ready. I slashed around before I even landed. I spun around, 360 degrees, cutting Dokkalfar in half. My sword went through them, slicing them like butter. I felt my vision take on a red tinge. It was like my family was lending me their power and courage. I finally realized who I was. After weeks of indecision, I felt empowered.

I let loose a battle cry and kept fighting. I quickly took down the elves closest to me. I sheathed my sword took out two long blades out of my boots and hacked away. I was a fierce and deadly force of nature. The Dokkalfar caught on and moved out of range of my blades. I sheathed them and pulled out two simple guns. I pushed off with my legs and flew through the air, shooting. I was confident that each bullet found its mark. As I landed, a bunch of Dokkalfar surrounded me. I pulled out my blades and defended myself. A few Ljosalfar came to aid.

"No, go cover your king," I insisted. I was the last of our leaders fighting. If I fell, the king would have to take over.

"He will not lose you as he lost your mother," one of them replied. I couldn't focus enough to understand the meaning behind his words. I cleared my head and pulled out my bow. I started shooting, making each arrow count. Out of the corner of my eyes, I saw the Dokkalfar king Ira retreating with his personal guard. I reached for an arrow but my sheath was empty. My blades were missing, somewhere on the battlefield, and my guns were out of ammo. All I had was my sword. Ira was over 100 yards away. I inhaled and pressed the button to set my sword on fire. I held it like a throwing knife. I exhaled calmly, holding on to my last hope. I prayed for strength and threw the sword.

I couldn't believe that it flew true. It pierced the king's heart. Ira disintegrated and his crown hit the ground. It was absurd that I was worried. I was, however, weaponless and defenseless. I didn't know how badly I was wounded. I couldn't feel the pain through the adrenaline. I steeled myself, preparing for hand-to-hand combat. I tossed my head back and felt blood splatter my face when my hair touched it. I raised my hands to cover my face.

My worry was unnecessary. The army fled with Ira's death. I felt the adrenaline fade and I swayed. I sat down and dropped my empty quiver.

"Miss Andrea," someone said. I looked up but couldn't tell who I was looking at. Whoever it was surveyed me once and picked me up. "You're safe. The battle is over. We won," he informed me.

"Where are you taking me?" I tried to demand. My voice sounded horrible. I dismissed the thought.

"The facility. You can rest. You're safe with me." The man carried me to a jeep and laid me in the backseat.

"Ric? Ollie?" I breathed questioningly.

"They're being taken to the facility as well," the man's calm voice informed me. A while later he picked me up out of the jeep and carried me into the facility. It should have bothered me that a stranger was carrying me but I couldn't think straight. He laid me on a bed in the infirmary and healers surrounded me. They shot something into my arm and I went out like a light.

21

I didn't know when I woke up but I felt sore all over. I was in my underclothes and a sheet covered me. I was stiff and alone.

"Excuse me," I croaked, my throat was dry.

Someone bustled over to me. "How do you feel, Miss Andrea?"

"Where is everyone?"

"Who would you like to see?"

"My brothers."

"Ric is in his study and Oliver in behind those curtains, still out cold, Miss." I stepped out of bed, slightly shaky. The coldness was uncomfortable on my bare skin. I pulled on a robe that was near my bed. It was papery and thin. The chill wasn't much better than before I put it on.

"Miss, you still need rest." I ignored the comment and marched, barefoot, to Ric's study. I opened the door to see him sitting behind the desk with Celine's daughter, Freya.

"Andrea," he breathed, getting up immediately. I realized I had no idea how I looked, whether I was macabre or decent. "You should be resting."

"I'm fine," I protested as he sat me in his chair. "Hi Freya," I cooed. Ric gave her to me and sat on the desk. He brushed my hair back and surveyed me with concern.

"How are you, Andrea?"

"I should be asking you that."

"I'm fine," he replied, his eyes tightening.

"What about the others?"

"Ollie's out cold but he'll be awake soon. Celine is healed, but resting – like you should be. Alex is making some arrangements."

"What arrangements? What about Eli?" I pressed.

"Funeral arrangements," he said, taking back Freya.

"How many warriors did we lose?"

"Only one."

"Who?" I pressed, annoyed that I had to push so hard.

"Eli," he whispered, his voice as soft as the wind.

"Ohh," I breathed. I rose from the chair.

"Andrea, where are you going?" Ric asked. I barely heard him over the ringing in my ears. I felt moisture in my eyes. I stumbled out of the room and looked for Eli. It made sense that he would be in the infirmary. I marched in authoritatively. I hoped my cover wouldn't be blown.

"Can we help you?" a woman asked.

"Where is he?" I demanded, my voice breaking.

"I'm sorry miss," she began.

"I want to see him!" I screamed, my voice ripping through an octave.

"We can't let you through."

"I'm Andrea Morgan!" I explained. I thought they couldn't recognize me. "Let me see him! Show him to me!" two soldiers restrained me and I struggled against them through my screams and tears.

"Get your hands off her," a clear voice ordered. I looked up to see Alex. His eyes were red-rimmed but his voice demanded respect. "Do you know who she is?" he demanded.

The soldiers let go of me and I stumbled to Alex. He led me into the room. Eli's body lay on the bed. He looked so peaceful, that I thought he might be asleep. My tears suddenly stopped and my legs moved of their own accord. I touched his cheek lightly and shivered. His skin was ice cold. He was really gone. I was having a hard time breathing. I felt the room spin and my eyes dropped closed. I felt a pair of steady arms catch me.

"Andrea!" Alex exclaimed. I felt him pick me up and carry me to a bed. "Hey look at me. Ric will kill me if I let something happen to you on my watch. C'mon, Andrea."

"Alex," I whispered.

"Hey, I'm here. I'm here," he soothed. He hugged me gently. I struggled to regain my composure. I couldn't be seen like this in public.

"He's gone," I breathed. Someone drew the curtains back a few inches and stuck their head in. Oliver peeked in.

"Ollie!" I exclaimed.

"Andie, hey. Wait, what's wrong?" he asked, looking me over.

"Eli's gone," I said, the words bringing a fresh round of tears. I saw Oliver's eyes darken too. "When's the funeral?" I asked.

"Tomorrow," Alex replied.

"What can I do?"

"You need to rest and heal."

"I can do that later. What can I do to help?"

Alex chewed on his lower lip, contemplating. "Okay... go out back and arrange the viewing area. It all has to be silver and gold."

"It's a funeral, Alex. Shouldn't the decorations be black?"

"Eli hated the stereotypical black funerals. I don't want to do something he wouldn't like. I don't want a single bit of black at his funeral."

"I'm on it. Silver and gold."

I went upstairs to get dressed first. I showered and pulled on one of Eli's T-shirts over my shorts. Then, I went out back where people were working hard. I instructed them on how to prepare the raised platform and then the arrangement of chairs around and in front of it. I was told that Eli's parents were coming. I remembered that his dad was Lilian's brother. That made them my aunt and uncle. I made sure two chairs were added for them around the platform.

Then, I went upstairs to pick out a dress. I had a wide variety of black to choose from but only came up with two silver dresses. I had to make sure it was decent enough to meet my aunt and uncle for the first time but also wolfy enough to appear in front of the pack. I decided on a gentle silver number that was both opaque and transparent. It would be fitted until my waist and straightened out until the floor. The dress looked like something I would wear to a prom. It was full-sleeved and had a cut-out on the back. I found a pair of silver heels to go with it. I set them out and went to Oliver's room. I knocked on the door gently, not wanting to wake him.

"Come in," he called. I opened the door and saw Oliver and Ric on the bed.

"C'mere," Ric invited gently. I laid with my head in his lap and my legs in Oliver's. Ric brushed my hair out of my face. "How are you?"

I shrugged. "What about you?"

"He was my best friend," Ric stated. "I miss him so much." I sat up to hug him and Oliver joined us. It felt good to cry with them. The three of us fell asleep in Oliver's room.

I woke up to Ric shaking my shoulder. "Andrea, come on. You have to go get dressed." I sat up so fast my head spun. I took a few deep breaths and got out of the bed. I went to my room and showered, I pulled on my dress and then brushed my hair into an intricately twisted and braided bun. I brushed on some waterproof makeup and put on my jewelry. I stepped into my pumps and looked in the mirror. The dress looked inappropriate for a funeral but I was relieved I didn't have to wear a veil. I opened the door of my room and saw Ric, looking like he was about to knock.

"Andie, I was about to knock. Jack's here. So are Eli's parents. Their names are Alice and Marcel. You should go meet them."

"Okay," I agreed.

"I'll introduce you to them." I took his arm lightly and he led me downstairs. Jack saw me before I saw him.

"Andie," he called relief saturating his voice. He extended his arms to me and I immediately let go of Ric. I ran into Jack's arms, throwing my arms around him. He hugged me tight. "I'm so sorry," he lamented. "I'm relieved you're okay though." I hugged him tighter.

"Andrea, I'm sorry. We have to go," Ric interrupted. I let go of Jack.

"Where are you going?" he asked.

"To see Eli's parents," I replied. He nodded as Ric led me to a room off the hall. Two people were inside, trying to comfort each other.

"Aunt Alice, Uncle Marcel," Ric greeted. "I'm so sorry for your loss." They looked up and glanced at Ric. Then, they focused on me and their eyes widened.

"Lily," Marcel gasped.

"Uncle Marcel, this is Andrea. My sister. Lilian's daughter."

"Hi," I said shyly.

"Ohh, it's so nice to meet you dear. You look so much like her. So beautiful."

"It's nice to meet you too," I said, shaking his hand.

"Shall we head out?" Ric asked smoothly.

Eli's parents stood up and I took Ric's arm again. We led them out to where the funeral was. I showed them to their seats. The rest of the chairs filled up soon. It was time to bring out the coffin. Ric, Celine, Alex, and I were going to be pallbearers. Ric and I excused ourselves and went to the hall of alphas. Celine and Alex were waiting for us. Oliver was downstairs.

"Alice and Marcel are here," Ric told them. Ric and I took the front while Celine and Alex were in the back of the coffin. We lifted Eli onto our shoulders. We carried him down, our heads held high in respect. The entire gathering stood as we set him down. Alice's grief was beyond tears while Marcel's flowed freely. In their defense, I had carefully composed myself and swore I wouldn't embarrass myself. But, I was a ticking time bomb. Anything could set me off.

After everyone sat down, Ric stood up.

"We are gathered here today to pay our final respects to Eli. He was a brave warrior and a loyal friend. He was my best friend and brother. May he find peace in Valhalla," Ric said.

I stood up next. I wasn't sure what to say, but I had to say something. "I'm Andrea and..." I stammered. I looked at Ric and he nodded in encouragement. "Eli didn't deserve to die. If I was a better warrior he wouldn't have. I should have been able to cover him on the battlefield. He should be here, laughing and talking. If I was a faster shooter, he would be alive," I lamented, breaking down in tears. Oliver stood up and enfolded me in his arms, letting me ruin his shirt. He helped me sit back down. I cried throughout the rest of the funeral and then staggered up to my room and cried some more. I had barely known Eli for more than a month but his death crippled me.

Ric walked in and helped me sit up. "Andrea, it's not your fault. Eli wouldn't have blamed you for his death."

"But I do," I cried.

"It's not what he would have wanted. We have to honor him."

"I will," I swore as I leaned into my brother's arms.

About The Author

Lekhaa MeenakshiSundaram is a young and ambitious writer who published her first book *The Werewolves of Brooklyn : Siege of the Dokkalfar* as she began her college life. It was always her dream to become a writer. She grew up reading books of various genres which naturally led to her discovering her passion for writing. She has always been a lover of all things supernatural and often finds herself revolving around the world of fantasy and fiction.

She has a personal blog titled *I Just Wanna Be A Girl.* You can find it at https://ijustwannabeagirl.blogspot.com/.